One Boy's Wish,
Two Men Answer

Series: Forever His Destiny Series

Book: 2

By

Nathan Leigh Moffett

Table of Contents

ACKNOWLEDGEMENT

I must offer my thanks to the Almighty God of the Bible, YAHWEH, who guided this entire journey. He provided the dreams, the visions, and the daily insights that shaped every page. This book is a testimony to His faithfulness—I am merely the pen in His hand.

PROLOGUE — GABRIEL'S POV

I didn't expect peace to feel this loud.

Crowds moved in waves around me—families, cast members, costumed performers, the rhythmic swell of music rising from the courtyard. Disney always had a way of swallowing chaos and turning it into choreography. People saw magic. Wonder. Escapism. They came for fantasy.

I was here for him.

Nathan walked three steps ahead of me, holding an armful of folders, maps, and color-coded binders like he'd been born for this place. His badge caught the sunlight—*Enchantment Realms Division. Chief Director & President.* His first day in a role he never imagined, and I never thought he'd take. He did, and it ranked and paid well beyond the role he would have had in the company he had trained for previously.

He glanced back at me, eyes bright with a nervous excitement that didn't belong to the man trapped in a workshop with a lunatic days earlier. That man still lived inside him… but here? He was lighter. Hopeful.

He smiled.

And for a moment, I forgot how to breathe.

I used to believe danger would always find him. That my shadow would follow him no matter where he went. But today— watching him walk into a dream he built on his own—I wondered if maybe, for once, his world didn't need protecting.

Maybe it just needed witnessing.

Nathan was trying to carry everything himself again. Always doing too much, stretching too far, proving he could stand on his own. I admired it. I hated it. I wanted to take every binder out of his hands, every burden out of his heart, and tell him that he no longer needed to do anything alone.

But I stayed quiet. He needed to feel this moment. And I needed to see it.

He stopped under the archway of the castle—the same castle where millions of wishes were whispered into the sky. He looked up as if he had something new to wish for. I could almost hear it. I could almost feel it.

He didn't know that I'd already decided.

I wasn't a man who believed in fairy tales. I believed in weaponry, in strategy, in the geometry of survival. I believed in keeping people alive, even when I had to lose myself to do it. I never believed in destiny.

But Nathan changed that.

He turned to me again, brushing hair out of his face, sunlight catching the corners of his smile.

"I can't believe this is real," he said. His voice trembled—not from fear, but from awe.

It occurred to me in that instant that I had never brought someone into my future. Not really. I had partners, allies, lovers… but no one I wanted beside me when everything went quiet, and I had nothing left to fight.

But here, in the shadow of a castle built on the promise of dreams, I understood something I had been too afraid to name:

Nathan wasn't just someone I wanted to protect. He was someone I wanted to build a life with.

A real one.

Not a life made of weapons or strategy or revenge. A life with mornings, and laughter, and arguments over where to hang ridiculous framed photos of cartoon mice. A life where I didn't wake up preparing for war.

A life where I could finally be a man—and not just a shield.

Nathan breathed in deeply, letting it out like he was releasing the last of his fear. "I feel like something big is coming," he murmured.

I did too. But he didn't know that "something big" had nothing to do with lives hanging in the balance, or did it?

It had to do with a ring in my pocket.

It had to do with a question I never imagined I'd be brave enough to ask.

And it had to do with a promise I made quietly to myself in the dark hours after the workshop terror— that I would stop running from the things I wanted, and stop pretending I didn't want him.

Nathan took a step forward into his new world.

I followed.

But for the first time in my life… I wasn't leading.

I was choosing.

And I knew—whether the universe blessed me or broke me for it—my next steps would belong to him.

Nathan was already thirty feet ahead of us, energized by caffeine, ambition, and an imagination that could bend reality into color.

"Over there, Henrik!" he yelled, pointing at a cluster of old trees near the bridge. "We'll have to clear a few of those and carve out a little cove so people can gather, take pictures, and go *gaga* over the new Enchantment Realm once it opens. It should feel like a reveal — like the world shifts when you cross that bridge."

Henrik Vann — Nathan's personal assistant, scheduling guardian, detail mule, and sometimes unwilling emotional support human — scribbled furiously.

He'd been chosen from a candidate pool of nearly two thousand applicants—men and women of every age and background—most of whom folded, cracked, or outright unraveled during the hiring gauntlet.

For three grueling days, the candidates endured interviews, memory trials, itinerary challenges, color-coordination tests, travel-booking simulations, crisis phone-call drills, shadowing assignments, and every other impossible task imaginable. All so Nathan could focus on creating magic at Disney—without drowning in the mundane chaos of administrative work.

Watching the process had felt less like recruitment and more like witnessing a condensed *Squid Game* marathon—minus the fatalities, though the emotional casualties were real enough.

Truth be told, I was relieved these duties fell to Henrik and not someone else. Nobody alive could manage Nathan's hurricane-brain the way Henrik could. And even then, Nathan often took over and added *more* tasks that hadn't existed five minutes earlier.

When Nathan wasn't in the room, Henrik spoke like he was.

"'Nathan wants it this way,'" "'Nathan said this must be symmetrical,'" "'Nathan would never approve that color palette,'"

Constant, relentless, and completely accurate.

"Uh-huh…" Henrik muttered now, half to himself, while writing so fast that smoke might've risen from the page. His mind was already juggling: park modification forms, architect drafts, safety restrictions, scheduled closures, signature routes, security notifications, roadway requests, pavement requirements, handrail placement, construction logistics — and at least seven things Nathan hadn't invented yet.

Finally, Henrik groaned. "Anything else?"

Nathan grinned like a troublemaker in a fairy-tale kingdom.

"I'm sure there will be. Why, Henrik? Already got a bunch shoved up your g-string?" He clapped him on the shoulder. "Relax. Pull up your big-girl panties and follow me. I *told* you there'd be a lot. I'm the visionary, and the Enchantment Realm has to be perfect. This is the park of dreams."

I smirked and walked the other direction after hearing all that. I wanted to get busy on a task I had in the wings, so to speak. And as ridiculous as the exchange sounded… Nathan meant every word.

He wanted to make something magical — for the park, for himself, for the world. And even though he hadn't proven anything yet, I could see it already.

Surely, what he was about to do would change everything.

Including me.

(1) THE RING, THE MOMENT, THE CHOICES

Peace didn't arrive quietly. It came with fireworks.

Not literal ones—though Disney had plenty of those—but the kind that went off in your chest when you saw someone you love step into the world they deserved.

Nathan walked ahead of me through the courtyard of the park, sunlight catching on the edge of his badge. *Enchanted Realm Division, Director & President.* His new title. His new life. His new beginning.

And if I had my way… the beginning of ours.

I watched him navigate his first day with that trademark mixture of confidence and uncertainty. He carried too many folders at once, made too many verbal notes, overstepped out of excitement, apologized instantly, then laughed at himself. I memorized every detail.

I wasn't looking for the right moment to propose. I was learning from him. In real time. The rhythms of his joy. The subtle tremors of his fears. The way his hands shook when something meant more than he wanted to admit.

But designing the ring—that took me to places inside myself I didn't know I had.

Three nights. Forty-one drafts. Six hours of metallurgy research. And exactly one panic attack.

I thought weapons were complicated. Turns out jewelry—the symbolism of it—is worse.

A ruby for July. Birthstones matter to him. He has admitted that without admitting it. A small superstitious part of him loves that his birth month is marked by a gem associated with courage.

The ruby chose itself.

Diamonds came next, but not as decoration. They were map points. Each one was a moment in his life that shaped him. His grandparents, his mother, his father, Hailey, Marcus, and… me.

Then came the crest.

A Batman-inspired emblem, yes, but not a direct copy. My version would be elegant. Architectural. Black platinum wings protecting the ruby from above—not overtly overshadowing it. Like him and me.

Myths can protect a person. But reality—the people who choose you—protects you more.

I wanted the ring to honor both.

Bill showed up uninvited.

I'd been hunched over the desk for hours, red stones and sketches scattered everywhere, when his massive silhouette filled my doorway.

"You're doing that thing again," he grumbled.

"What thing?" I didn't look up.

He stepped closer and tapped the table. "The thing where your jaw locks, your shoulders go up to your ears, and you pretend you're not terrified."

I sighed. "I'm designing a ring, not defusing a bomb."

He laughed once. "You look more stressed than when you *were* defusing bombs."

He picked up one of the drafts. "Why so many versions of wings?"

"It's symbolic."

"Of what? That you're a bat? A bird? A—"

"It's for Nathan."

Bill stopped talking instantly. His whole-body language changed.

"Oh." He lowered the paper and exhaled. "Ohhh."

"Not that." I corrected quickly. "Not yet."

"You're gonna do it," he said, completely ignoring me. "You're actually gonna propose."

"Possibly," I muttered. "Maybe. Eventually."

Bill sat down across from me like he was preparing to negotiate a hostage release.

"Look, Gabe… you're not good at subtlety. You plan things. You execute. You win. This—" He gestured at the ring sketches. "This isn't execution. This is a vulnerability. And you suck at vulnerability."

I glared. He shrugged.

He wasn't wrong.

He leaned in. "When you give him this, don't think like a soldier. Think like a man who has something worth living for."

Something inside me cracked at that.

"And for the record?" he added. "He's gonna say yes."

"How do you know?"

"Because he loves you," Bill said simply. "Not your bank account. Not your muscles. Not your scars. *You.*"

I swallowed hard.

Bill rose from the chair with a grunt, clapping a hand on my shoulder— a hand roughly the size and density of a cast-iron skillet. The impact nearly rocked me out of the stool.

"Stop staring at that ruby like it committed a felony," he said, "Finish the damn ring."

I huffed a laugh, unable to argue with him.

Goldberg paused in the doorway, scratching at his beard with mild suspicion.

"Oh — and by the way," he added casually, "pretty sure I saw Nathan heading this direction." He lowered his voice conspiratorially. "Kid's got a sixth sense for when you're up to something. I think he smells a proposal."

My heartbeat spiked.

Bill smirked, satisfied he'd stirred the pot, and gave the doorframe a light punch for good measure.

"Good luck, Romeo."

And just like that, he was gone.

Henrik was everywhere Nathan was, almost. He was so sharp, graceful, and observant to an almost unsettling degree. There was a quiet intensity about him that reminded me, uncomfortably, of myself at nineteen.

I caught Henrik backstage after a planning meeting for a new Disney special-needs initiative—an ambitious cooperative designed to help kids experience the Magic Kingdom with the same joy, freedom, and wonder as everyone else.

"Mr. Michaels," he greeted politely.

"Henrik," I spoke quietly, and hurried him away from the crowds. "I need your insight."

This startled him. His eyebrows rose slightly. "About Nathan?"

"Yes."

"His dietary restrictions, his sleep cycle, or the way he likes his iced drinks, depending on mood?" he asked earnestly.

I blinked. "I… already know those."

Henrik smiled. "Good. Then what do you wish to know from me?"

"What makes him feel safe?" It slipped out before I could stop it.

Henrik softened immediately. "Ah. Something really important."

"Yes."

He folded his hands thoughtfully. "Nathan fears abandonment more than any danger known to man. He worries he will be 'too much' sometimes. Too emotional. Too exhausted. Too human. He hides it well."

I felt something twist in my chest.

Henrik continued, "If you are planning something important, Gabriel… understand this: he does not need the perfect moment. He needs the honest one."

I exhaled through my nose. That was… too accurate.

"Also," Henrik added quietly, "he wants to choose you, but he wants to be certain you are choosing him—*not your fear of losing him.*"

That hit deeper than I expected.

I thanked him. He bowed slightly. And I left knowing exactly what to do.

Nathan is emotional and intuitive. He will overanalyze silence and celebrate the smallest word. He remembers moments others forget. He connects meanings no one else sees.

So, I had to choose a moment worthy of him.

But I also had to choose a moment that he wouldn't anticipate.

He loves Disney magic. He loves the wishing lanterns. He loves the fountain. He loves the symbolism of stars.

But more than anything— He loves when love is real, not staged.

He once told Hailey (and I overheard):

"When someone chooses you with their whole being, you feel it. You don't ever ignore it."

So yes, I would do it by the fountain where the lights softened everything. Where water reflected the sky. Where crowds thinned, and the world held its breath.

But not with spectacle. Not with performers. Not with fireworks.

Just me. Him. And a ring that held our story.

The moment I chose was sunset—when gold melts into violet, when the day exhales, when the world shifts from reality to magic.

The one moment he always paused to look at the sky, as if checking whether his wish was still there.

There are things I've never said aloud.

Nathan scares me. Not because he is dangerous. But because he is *good.*

Too good. Too forgiving. Too hopeful. Too soft-hearted for someone like me.

And yet, he is also the bravest man I've ever known.

We put our lives in danger for each other. We bled for each other. We chose each other in the ugliest, darkest situations—when every instinct screamed to run.

So why would I not marry him? He's everything I've longed for and more.

He is not the fairytale hero. He is not the myth. He is the man who turned toward me instead of away.

The man who stood in front of a grenade and said, "I'm not leaving you."

The man who threw himself into the path of a bullet and swore, "It will never touch you—not while I breathe."

The man who risks, and breaks, and heals, and hopes… even when he's terrified.

I don't know every part of him. He doesn't know every part of me. But love isn't about knowing someone perfectly—it's about recognizing the truth in who they already are.

And I know him enough to know he's the one. I know he feels the same.

My life is about choosing him now— and tomorrow— and every day after that, even as we discover the pieces of each other, we haven't seen yet.

Because that's what love is: not certainty, but choosing anyway.

And I will choose him. Again and again.

Not because I have wealth. Not because I have power. Not because I have a name.

But because I have *him*.

And eternity together, if I'm lucky.

(2) The Ring, The Reveal, The Ruin

I didn't expect to feel nervous showing the ring to anyone—until all three of them were staring at me like they were waiting for me to pull the Ark of the Covenant out of my jacket.

Bill Goldberg crossed his arms, Hailey bounced in place, and Henrik—God help me—was already wiping beneath his eyes even though I hadn't even opened the box yet.

"Alright," I muttered, "but nobody touches it."

I opened the small black case.

The room inhaled.

The ruby glowed like captured fire. The black-platinum wings cradled it. Diamonds circled it like tiny constellations. My inscription curved inside the band, discreet and absolute.

Henrik immediately broke down. Not just a tear. Not just a sniffle.

A full emotional collapse.

"Oh—my—God," he whispered, voice cracking. "Mr. Michaels, this is… this is the most beautiful thing I've ever seen. He's going to—he's going to die. He's literally going to die. I would die. Why don't people propose to *me*? I'm nice. I'm organized. I color-code calendars—"

"Henrik," I warned.

He sniffled dramatically. "Sorry. I'm just… emotionally winded."

Hailey fanned him with a theme-park map. "Girl, breathe. Air is your friend."

Then there was Bill.

He leaned forward, squinting at the ring like it was a new piece of military hardware. "Kick-ass design," he said. "Just one question."

"No," I said instantly.

He kept going anyway. "Does it do anything? Nuclear strike? Targeting a laser? Napalm burst? Could it fire a bat-a-rang out the side if somebody pisses him off?"

Hailey snorted. "It probably has Wi-Fi."

Henrik dabbed his eyes. "It needs none of those things. It is perfection. *Perfection,*" he repeated for emphasis.

I closed the ring box carefully. "This is not a toy. It's not a weapon."

Bill shrugged. "Everything's a weapon if you throw it hard enough."

Hailey elbowed him. "He's being romantic, Bill."

"Yeah, well, romance should at least come with a self-destruct button."

I exhaled sharply. "He's ready. I'm ready. I just need the right moment."

"And when is that?" Hailey asked.

"Soon," I said quietly. "Tonight."

Henrik clapped like a proud fairy godmother. Bill smirked. Hailey squealed.

And I left before any of them could ruin my resolve.

I think Nathan knows something is up. He isn't oblivious. He never has been.

Even when I thought I was being subtle, he kept glancing at me sideways throughout the afternoon—little looks, little smiles, the kind that meant he knew I was hiding something and chose not to pry.

That's what he does. He respects my walls… even when he wants inside them.

He didn't ask questions. He didn't ruin the surprise.

But his eyes lingered on me longer than usual—as if he could sense that something in me was humming with expectation. I swear, if I didn't know any better, he's half-psychic.

He smiled the soft, trembling smile he gets when he's scared to hope for too much.

God, he had no idea how much he deserved.

Sunset arrived like a gift.

The sky went gold, then rose-pink, then violet. The fountain lights shimmered. Music drifted from the speakers—gentle, warm, inviting.

I had the ring in my pocket. My pulse was steady. My mind is clear.

He stood at the edge of the fountain, watching the way the light turned the water to liquid stars.

"I love this time of day," he said quietly. "Everything feels… possible."

I walked toward him, hand slipping into my jacket.

This was it. The moment.

"Nathan," I began, "there's something I—" but I was cut off mid-sentence by an abrupt and deafening piercing sound from above.

The sound cut through the air like a squeal from too much microphone in a speaker.

Then it had an annoying whistling which changed to a quick and sharp crackling, burning, and hell-fire snap of molten rock being burst open. It was not from this world. Not from a safe environment.

"Nathan—move!" I yelled. "It's headed right for us."

We bolted, still covering our ears. Something fiery, metallic, and vicious roared overhead—

Ten seconds, maybe less, and then we knew it would be a tremendous impact. We had sprinted away from the courtyard where the fountain rested, feet pounding the pavement as fast as we could to safety while the sky seemingly rained fragments.

The object crashed directly into the fountain. The explosion of steam and light blinded half the courtyard. Water erupted into the air and fragments of rock—or something like rock— splintered outward like shrapnel. We hit the ground behind a stone planter just as the impact rippled through the pavement.

People screamed. Security shouted. A glowing substance spread through the fountain like neon blood.

Nathan trembled beside me, gripping my arm. "I—I saw it," he whispered. "It fell right near where we were standing."

"I know," I breathed. "Stay low. Don't touch anything."

The object pulsed with heat, dripping molten glow into the water. Shards littered the perimeter, too bright, too alive to be natural.

But everyone was safe. Somehow, unbelievably safe.

I reached for my pocket.

Empty.

Cold shot through me.

No. No, no, no—The ring. The ring was gone.

I scrambled to my feet, scanning the pavement, the planter, the ground where I'd fallen—Nothing.

Panic clawed at my throat. Not for the ring alone—but because I didn't know if this place, this moment, this sudden alien impact—wasn't safe for Nathan.

He tugged at my sleeve. "Gabriel—don't go near it—"

"I have to find it…..something," I snapped, then softened instantly. "I have to… I need to find something that I need."

Nathan stared at me, eyes wide both with confusion and then unspoken understanding.

The sky still glowed. The object still pulsed. And somewhere in the chaos—My ring, *our* ring—the promise I had forged with my own hands—was gone. And I had no idea where it could have gone.

(3) THE RING AND THE FALL

The impact had thrown more than just shards of glowing debris across the courtyard. In the split seconds when the molten object slammed into the fountain, the shockwave dislodged the ring from Gabriel's hand. It tumbled across the pavement, skipped once, and slid toward the base of the shattered fountain where the anomaly's heat radiated in waves.

The ring came to a stop beside a fracture in the stone—so close to the molten core that its metal glinted under the unnatural light. For several seconds, the ruby and platinum crest rested against a stream of glowing substance leaking from the object. The heat did not melt the ring. Instead, the anomaly seemed to cling to it, tendrils of shimmering luminescence pulling toward the metal, as if drawn to its composition.

When emergency lights snapped on and security forces rushed to evacuate the courtyard, the ring went unnoticed. The crowd was moved back. Government vehicles arrived. Hazmat barriers were erected, and agents in protective suits formed a perimeter around the crash site.

Gabriel searched as much of the area as protocol would allow. He paced the outer perimeter, scanned storm drains, rubble, planters, and even the underside of benches. But he couldn't go close—not without clearance. Not without risk.

However, Gabriel Michaels was not without connections.

Within an hour, he secured authorization for limited access and a hazmat suit. It wasn't difficult. The right call, the right tone, and doors always opened for him. He didn't wait for an escort; he stepped over the safety barrier and entered the restricted zone on his own authority.

Inside the perimeter, the air shimmered with heat. Fragments of dark, metallic stone pulsed with faint light. The crater at the fountain's center glowed from within, casting flickering reflections across Gabriel's visor. He swept the area methodically, debris crunching beneath his boots. The ring was small—easily overlooked.

And just as all hope was dwindling for Gabriel, fate allowed a different outcome. Lying just out of normal eyesight yet 'twinkling' for Gabriel to find it, he was drawn to it.

It lay half-buried beneath a curled plate of impact metal, the ruby glowing faintly in violation of all-natural law. The black-platinum wings of the crest carried an iridescent sheen they had not possessed before, as if the metal itself had inhaled something from the fallen object.

The moment Gabriel touched it, the faint luminescence retreated inward—absorbed by the ring, as though hiding.

"Ah, I've been looking for you everywhere, little man." I exhaled, lifting the ring carefully with gloved fingers. Heat pulsed through the metal—subtle, but unmistakable. "Still… I need to be sure you're not dangerous."

The ruby glowed faintly, then dimmed. Not random. Reactive.

"That's not reassuring," I murmured. "And you're not going anywhere near Nathan until I know you won't harm him."

I slipped the ring into a sealed containment capsule clipped to my belt, double-locking it. Even then, I didn't feel comfortable walking more than ten steps with the thing.

Once I cleared the perimeter, I stripped off the hazmat suit, transferred the capsule to a secure case, and headed for one of my off-record facilities—a lab very few people had access to.

Mr. Emerson was already there when I arrived.

He stood beside the examination chamber, arms folded, expression unreadable as always. "You retrieved it?"

"Yes." I placed the secure case on the counter with care. "It must have made contact with the anomaly because it seems to glow or pulse at times."

His eyebrow twitched—his version of shock. "That is… concerning."

"Which is why I need every scan you have," I said. "Spectrometry, radiation, molecular integrity, alien particulate checks—everything."

"And the emotional reason?" he asked dryly.

I didn't answer.

He sighed. "Very well. Let's begin."

I opened the case.

Light spilled out—soft, pulsing, alive.

Emerson stepped back. "Gabriel… whatever that ring absorbed… it isn't just radiation."

Emerson leaned forward, but not too close. Behind the glass of the containment field, the ring gave a slow pulse—almost like a heartbeat, but faint, mechanical, wrong.

"It's responding," Emerson muttered.

"To what?" I asked.

He didn't answer immediately. Instead, he stepped to the side console and replayed the last thirty seconds of audio—the portion of our conversation when we were discussing contamination. The waveform on the screen shifted…and the ring's glow flickered in sync with it.

Emerson's frown deepened.

"It's… listening," he said carefully. "Interpreting our voices. Not in any linguistic sense I can decode, but… It's reacting to patterns. Frequency. Tone."

The ring pulsed twice, almost like it was acknowledging him.

I stiffened. "Don't anthropomorphize it."

"I'm not," he said quietly. "I'm stating a fact."

Emerson brought up a new scanner. The chamber filled with a soft hum, and the ring's glow intensified as though answering the machine's vibration. A pulse of light shimmered through the ruby, refracting in unnatural branching patterns like tiny circuits woven beneath the gem.

"What is it doing?" I demanded.

Emerson typed rapidly, watching streams of data spill across his screens. "It's translating."

"Translating what?"

"Our sound." He looked at me, unsettled. "It's trying to… communicate."

The chamber hummed again.

This time, the ring hummed back. Not loudly. Not aggressively. But clearly. A tone—bright, metallic, harmonic—vibrated through the glass.

I stepped closer. "Emerson."

"I know," he murmured.

"Is it dangerous?"

He lifted the containment tablet, running the ring through more tests—thermal, molecular, frequency analysis, energy absorption rates.

Each time the machine emitted a pulse, the ring responded with its own: shorter, softer, as if it were testing its voice.

After a long silence, Emerson finally said, "Let's run a full diagnostic."

We did. For ninety minutes.

Tests I didn't even have names for. Energy mapping. Spectral behavior. Interference resonance. Biofeedback anomalies. Molecular density fluctuations.

The ring reacted to every scan—but never predictably.

At the ninety-four-minute mark, Emerson set down his tablet.

"We've confirmed it has new abilities," he said. "Not just contamination. Alteration."

"What kind of abilities?"

He shook his head slowly—an expression I had seen only when he stood over impossible intelligence files. "I don't know the extent of the abilities."

"That's not an answer."

"It's the only one I have."

I stared at the ring.

The ruby seemed deeper now—like the glow had sunk beneath the surface, burrowing into the stone itself. It no longer pulsed visibly, but I could feel something radiating from it.

A quiet awareness.

Almost… curiosity.

Emerson spoke again, voice low. "Gabriel, I have no idea why that object—whatever it was—chose to interact with your ring.

And I have no explanation for why the metal absorbed the anomaly instead of melting."

He hesitated. Emerson never hesitated.

"I cannot tell you if it poses a threat."

My chest tightened.

Nathan.

Nathan, who would have worn that ring on his hand. Nathan, who would have trusted me when I slid it onto his finger. Nathan, who believed I would never let anything harm him.

Emerson must have read something in my silence because he pressed his palm to the console, locking the containment chamber.

"Gabriel," he warned, "you cannot give this to Nathan."

I didn't answer.

Not because I disagreed.

Not because I was reckless.

But because something inside me couldn't ignore the truth:

If this ring changed because it made contact with the anomaly… and if that anomaly fell in front of us… Then it had chosen our path.

Not Nathan's. Not mine.

Ours.

But that truth terrified me more than anything.

Because now, I had a ring with unknown abilities, an alien contamination of unknown intention—and a man I loved more than my own life.

And I had no idea how to protect him from either.

(4) THE SECOND EVENT

Nathan called Gabriel twice on his mobile.

The first time, the call went straight to voicemail. The second time, Gabriel answered—but only with a quiet, "I'll be there soon."

Nathan knew that tone. It was the tone Gabriel used when something was wrong, but he wasn't ready to say what it was.

Nathan waited near the service corridor outside the castle courtyard, arms wrapped around himself. The night air felt colder than usual, though the breeze carried warmth from the lingering magic of the park. People had begun returning after the crash, reassured by the government's fast containment, but Nathan's stomach hadn't settled.

He paced.

He didn't want to pry. He didn't want to ruin a surprise. He didn't want to pressure Gabriel.

But he could feel it in his bones—Gabriel was hiding something. And whatever it was, it wasn't small.

Gabriel approached with that measured stride of his—calm on the surface, storm underneath. Nathan saw it instantly. The eyes. The breath. The tension in his shoulders. Something had happened.

"Gabriel?" Nathan asked softly. "Talk to me."

Gabriel didn't answer at first. He scanned rooftops, doorways, even the sky—old habits resurfacing only when he sensed a threat.

Finally, he exhaled. "I shouldn't have gone that close," he said. "But I had to retrieve something."

"Something of interest?" Nathan echoed. "Or something so important you gambled with your life?"

Gabriel's silence confirmed everything.

Nathan stepped closer. "I know you. You think you hide things well, but not from me." His voice trembled slightly. "What was so important you risked going near that thing—and for so long? I've been here for hours telling the press nothing went wrong and that the fountain will be fixed soon."

Gabriel hesitated, just long enough for Nathan to understand: It wasn't just important. It was personal.

Before Gabriel could answer, engines cut through the quiet.

Black SUVs. Unmarked. Government plates.

Nathan's pulse spiked.

Gabriel turned sharply toward the vehicles, hand twitching toward where a weapon would normally be. "Stay behind me," he murmured.

Four agents emerged in tactical black. One wore a badge Nathan didn't recognize— But Gabriel did.

His whole posture tightened.

The lead agent removed her helmet. A woman stood beneath it, hair braided tight, eyes hard as tempered steel.

"Gabriel Michaels," she said. "It's been a long time."

Nathan felt the shift in Gabriel—dread, anger, and something else… something old.

"Commander Reyna Voss," Gabriel replied.

Nathan had never heard the name.

Voss stepped forward. "We intercepted transmissions from inside your private lab. Alien-coded signals. Encrypted frequencies. Something is communicating—and you are holding an unregistered object from the site."

Nathan looked sharply at Gabriel. "Alien object?"

Gabriel didn't blink. "I retrieved nothing," he said.

Voss gave a humorless smile. "You forget who trained you. Your tells haven't changed."

Nathan saw it—the faint shift in Gabriel's jaw. He was hiding something.

"We want immediate access," Voss said, "to whatever you extracted."

Gabriel stepped forward. "It's contained. Safe."

"Safe?" She scoffed. "We traced communication spikes to the exact moment you entered your lab. Whatever you're analyzing is not dormant."

Nathan's breath caught. "Communicating?"

Gabriel shut his eyes briefly—confirmation in silence.

"Step aside," Voss ordered. "We'll take it from here."

"No," Gabriel said quietly.

The word sliced the air. Nathan had never heard such controlled refusal.

"You don't understand what you're dealing with," Voss warned.

"I understand enough to know what it will not become," Gabriel replied. "And it is not going into government storage or weapons development."

"Then give me the object," Voss said.

Gabriel didn't move.

"Detain him," she ordered.

Agents stepped forward— And the park lights flickered.

Once. Twice. Then all of them blew out, plunging everything into darkness.

Nathan gasped. "What's happening—"

A pulse rippled from Gabriel's pocket. A deep, metallic bell-tone—alien and electric.

The ring.

The ground vibrated. The air shimmered. The fountain erupted with blinding white light as water shot upward like gravity had reversed.

"Fall back!" Voss shouted.

Nathan grabbed Gabriel's arm. Gabriel reached into his pocket—

And the ring ignited.

Not fire. Not molten drip. A crystalline, spiraling current of energy that tore upward like a column through space.

A second object appeared in the sky— silent, massive.

Nathan whispered, horrified, "Gabriel… please tell me that's not another one."

"No," Gabriel said, heart pounding. "It's something else."

The object split open like a flower of metal and light— and sent a beam straight toward the fountain.

People screamed. Agents dove for cover. Sirens wailed.

Gabriel pulled Nathan behind a stone pillar as the second event detonated with a rippling shockwave.

Through it all— The ring whispered in pulses. A response.

(5) THE CONNECTION

The second anomaly hovered above the ruined fountain, plates shifting, seams glowing. Smaller than the first, but sharper—focused, searching.

And it found what it wanted.

The ring in Gabriel's hand pulsed, answering with soft harmonic tones.

Nathan instinctively gripped Gabriel's arm. "Gabriel… It's communicating with it."

Gabriel stared at the ring as if seeing it anew.

The anomaly emitted a beam that swept the courtyard. When it touched the ring, the structure chimed—melodic, eerie. Not random. Not hostile. Calling.

And the ring answered.

The ruby glowed, black-platinum wings shifting with blue patterns—translating something unseen.

The air thickened. Nathan's arms prickled. "What does it want?" he whispered.

Gabriel finally spoke. "To understand the… bond between us."

Nathan blinked. "What bond?"

"The one that pulled us together in the workshop," Gabriel said. "That kept us alive. The one that's been… growing."

The anomaly chimed again. The ring pulsed in reply—

And the world erupted.

"Seize that object!" Voss shouted.

Agents surged forward.

The ring reacted first.

A shockwave burst outward—not destructive, but commanding. Electric arcs snapped against weapons, frying radios and earpieces.

Nathan gasped. "It's—defending itself."

Gabriel shook his head. "No. It's defending us."

"Fall back!" Voss yelled. "Do not engage the artifact!"

Some obeyed. Others pressed forward.

The anomaly woke fully now—panels shifting, light rippling like liquid lightning. Angry.

The ring flared with gold-white light. Intricate glyphs spiraled across its surface, harmonizing with the anomaly.

They spoke.

Not words— pulses. Intervals. Mathematical sequences. Two minds exchanging entire languages in seconds.

Nathan stared. "Gabriel… the ring is talking to it."

"Or remembering it," Gabriel whispered.

Another pulse—almost pleading.

Nathan grabbed Gabriel's hand. The ring's glow shifted—warmer, steadier.

"It responds to us," Gabriel breathed. "To our connection."

Nathan flushed. Gabriel noticed. So did the anomaly.

The connection intensified—

Voss moved.

In one fluid motion, the ring tore from Gabriel's fingers, yanked by an unseen force into a matte-black containment cube Voss snapped shut. She never touched it.

Another agent captured the anomaly the same way. Both cubes sealed with a metallic snap.

Inside, each object pulsed—slower, muted, but still answering one another.

Separated. Shielded. Still talking.

Voss approached Gabriel, expression hardened by duty and old history.

"You had no right to retrieve alien material."

"You trained me to assess threats," Gabriel said. "It was a threat until I secured it."

"You should've turned it over."

"I don't answer to command anymore."

Her jaw tightened. "You walked away. Disappeared. Eight people thought you were dead."

Nathan froze. He had never heard any of this.

"We were a team," Voss continued. "You abandoned us."

"It was necessary," Gabriel said.

"For who?" she demanded. "For you—or the people you were trying to protect?"

Gabriel didn't answer.

Nathan's chest ached for him.

Voss exhaled. "The artifacts are broadcasting bursts we can't decode. We traced the first spikes to your private lab."

Nathan's stomach dropped. Gabriel had kept that from him.

Two agents flanked Gabriel. Two stepped toward Nathan.

"Hey—what is this?" Nathan protested.

"Protocol," one agent answered. "You're both involved."

Gabriel didn't struggle, but his voice went lethal. "You touch him again, and you'll regret it."

The agents faltered. Voss did not.

"You're both part of an active alien-contact investigation," she said. "And you—" she pointed at Gabriel—"may be compromised."

"Compromised?" Nathan repeated.

"I'm fine," Gabriel said through clenched teeth.

"You retrieved something that interacted with the anomaly," Voss said. "That makes you a vector until proven otherwise."

"Retrieved what?" Nathan demanded.

"We don't know yet," Voss replied.

Gabriel inhaled. "Nathan. Stay behind me."

Nathan did not because of fear, but because Gabriel had shifted into something fierce, absolute, ready to break the world.

"Bring them," Voss ordered.

Before agents could move, a new vehicle screeched to a halt at the edge of the courtyard.

Mr. Emerson stepped out, flanked by three analysts and carrying a secured black case.

Voss turned, irritated. "You were cleared to come?"

"Yes," Emerson replied evenly. "And I have relevant data."

"You will share it," she said.

"In your presence," he agreed.

Emerson walked straight past the cluster of agents and stopped beside Gabriel and Nathan, as if the armed perimeter didn't exist.

"The ring," he said quietly, "is developing structured communication patterns. It's translating the anomaly's frequency. When you and Nathan interact physically, the translation stabilizes."

Nathan stared at him. "What does that mean?"

Emerson glanced at Voss, then at Gabriel, then at the two sealed cubes glowing faintly in opposite directions.

"It means," Emerson said cautiously, "the artifacts—both fragments—recognize something about the two of you."

"Recognize?" Voss pressed.

Emerson opened the case. A small holo-display flickered to life, lines of light forming two distinct pulsing waveforms.

"One anomaly," he said, pointing to the first pattern, "is attuned to Gabriel."

"And the other?" Voss asked.

Emerson looked directly at Nathan.

"It's attuned to him."

The courtyard fell utterly silent.

Even through layers of alloy and containment fields, the two anomalies seemed to pause— as if they, too, were listening.

(6) THE THREAD BETWEEN THEM

The armored vehicle jolted forward, its interior lit by cold blue strips along the ceiling. Nathan sat restrained across from Gabriel, their wrists not cuffed but locked into magnetic bands along the bench—"for safety," the agents claimed.

Gabriel didn't look angry. He looked calculating.

Nathan had seen this version of him only once before— the night in the warehouse when Gabriel had decided, silently and absolutely, that he would not let Nathan die.

"Are you alright?" Nathan whispered.

Gabriel lifted his eyes. A fraction softer. Only for him.

"Yes. Are you?"

"I don't like it when they take you away from me."

Gabriel's jaw tightened. "I don't either."

Across from them, Commander Voss sat rigid, arms folded, eyes sharp as blades—watching, evaluating, dissecting every exchange.

Nathan didn't understand the full history between her and Gabriel, but he understood tension when he felt it. Between the two of them, the air felt ready to crack.

Mr. Emerson sat beside Voss, tablet open, the holographic display showing two pulsing signatures—one gold-red, one blue-white—interweaving like strands of living DNA.

Nathan didn't miss the way the pulses shifted subtly every time he or Gabriel spoke.

It was undeniable now.

The anomalies responded to *them.*

Specifically, to them together.

The transport halted at a secured underground facility beneath the park—cold steel walls, reinforced blast doors, humming fluorescent lights. The air smelled of ionized metal and sterilized equipment.

Nathan and Gabriel were escorted to an interrogation chamber. Not threatening—but clinical.

One table. Two chairs. Mirrored wall. A ceiling camera glowed red.

Emerson entered first. Voss followed.

Agents took positions along the walls.

"Gabriel Michaels," Voss said, taking her seat. "You are to explain, in full, exactly what you saw and what the object reacted to when you made contact with it."

Gabriel didn't sit. He stood tall, centered, a fortress in human form.

"I already told you," he said. "I don't know."

Voss slammed her hand on the table. "Don't lie to me."

Nathan flinched.

Gabriel didn't.

"I don't lie," he said. "Not anymore." Voss's face flickered—pain, anger, betrayal—before hardening again.

"Fine," she snapped. "Then we'll begin with him."

Her gaze shifted sharply to Nathan.

Gabriel's posture changed instantly—a protective snap, like a wolf shifting between someone he trusts and someone he doesn't.

"No," Gabriel said coldly. "He's uninvolved."

Nathan's voice cracked softly. "Gabriel… I am involved."

A silence pulsed between them, painful and tender at once. Voss gestured. Agents moved.

"No—!" Gabriel surged forward, but three guards forced him back against the wall.

Nathan was guided to the chair.

"Don't hurt him," Gabriel growled, voice low, lethal.

Voss rolled her eyes. "We're not going to hurt your boyfriend."

Nathan's face turned scarlet. Gabriel's turned to stone. But before Voss could question him—

A siren wailed through the facility.

Every guard jerked upright. Voss's tablet flashed red. Emerson's device pinged with an alarm.

"What now?" Voss snapped.

Emerson stared at the data feed. "Commander… both anomalies are destabilizing."

Nathan's pulse spiked. "Destabilizing how?"

Before Emerson could answer, the lights flickered—lights dying, then flaring back to life.

On the hologram display, the two anomaly signatures were pulsing wildly, their once-harmonic patterns turning erratic, distorted, distressed.

Voss cursed. "They're not supposed to be active in containment."

"They're not," Emerson said. "Not physically." He turned slowly toward Nathan and Gabriel. "They're reacting through them."

The room fell silent.

Without warning—

Both Nathan and Gabriel gasped simultaneously.

A sound—No, a *frequency*—pierced the space between them. Not heard. Felt.

A vibration deep in the bones, the pulse of something ancient, searching, intelligent.

Nathan clutched his chest. "Gabriel—"

Gabriel staggered, grabbing the back of the chair. "I—feel it—"

Emerson's tablet lit up with cascading symbols— geometric shapes fractals glyphs mathematical sequences repeating in patterns that defied known physics.

Voss shouted, "GET A MEDICAL TEAM—"

"Wait!" Emerson barked. "It isn't harming them."

The symbols shifted again—aligning, condensing – forming something clearer. Words.

Not English. But something like language— constructed from mathematics and tone.

Nathan whispered, trembling, "It's… talking."

Gabriel, pale but focused, translated instinctively—not linguistically, but intuitively.

"It's asking," he said hoarsely. "Why are we apart?"

Nathan blinked. "Us?"

"No." Gabriel shook his head. "The anomalies. They want to know why *they* were separated."

The lights brightened—A second signal emerged. Softer. Almost mournful.

Nathan felt tears burn behind his eyes. "It's sad."

Gabriel swallowed hard. "Yes."

Voss's face turned white. "You're telling me these things have emotions?"

Emerson whispered, "It appears so."

"THIS IS AN INTERROGATION ROOM," Voss shouted. "NOT A DAMN THERAPY SESSION FOR METEORITES!"

But the anomalies ignored her.

Instead, the frequencies shifted again, faster now, forming something more direct.

A projection.

Blue light filled the room. Symbols floated in mid-air. A shape formed—two nodes connected by a luminous thread, constantly pulled toward each other no matter how far they moved apart.

Nathan stared. "It's showing us…"

Gabriel finished quietly:

"A bond."

Voss finally snapped. "THIS IS GETTING OUT OF CONTROL! PUT THEM BOTH IN SEPARATE HOLDING CELLS—"

The anomalies reacted instantly.

The facility shook. A violent pulse flared through the walls, melting light fixtures and exploding monitors. Guards fell to their knees. Electronics sputtered and died.

Nathan screamed. Gabriel lunged toward him.

The anomalies' message flashed one final time:

DO NOT SEPARATE THE PAIR.

Then everything went dark.

41

(7) THE INTERROGATION

Commander Voss was furious.

Not loud-furious. Not chaotic-furious.

Worse. Controlled fury.

Her jaw was set in a rigid line, her eyes sharp as scalpels, her voice cold enough to cut ice. The courtyard had been cleared, the anomalies locked in separate containment units behind her, both pulsing faintly—dim, watchful, disturbingly calm.

They were listening.

Nathan could feel it. Gabriel could, too. Even if Voss refused to acknowledge it.

"Let's proceed," Voss snapped. "Nathan, we're starting with you."

Gabriel stepped forward. "If you threaten him—"

"I'm not threatening him," Voss hissed. "I'm asking questions. Directly. Efficiently. And without your interference."

Nathan lifted a hand. "I'm not sure I have the answers you want, lady. I wasn't exactly on *your* radar the way you were on Gabriel's."

Gabriel's lips twitched. Voss's eye twitched harder.

"State your relationship to the anomaly," Voss demanded.

Nathan shrugged. "Well, we're strictly platonic—at the moment—but I am open to exploring our dynamic if, you know… it ever *rises to the occasion.*"

Voss blinked once. Slowly.

Gabriel coughed to hide a laugh. "Nathan…"

"What?" Nathan whispered. "She's being annoying, but I'm being cooperative."

"You're being… you," Gabriel muttered.

"Exactly."

Voss pressed on. "The anomaly responded to you. Why?"

Nathan raised a brow. "I mean… I *have* been known to flirt. Have you seen my smile recently? It's devastating."

A soft pulse came from Nathan's anomaly container.

It sounded suspiciously like amusement.

Voss stiffened. "Do not make jokes. This is a national security incident."

"It *is*?" Nathan echoed. "What is this, a reboot of *X-Files: The Discount Years*? Am I being filmed? Where's the hidden camera? And please tell me my hair has at least main-character energy right now."

He glanced at a lamp. "Do I need to stare dramatically into that for the big secret-camera reveal? Oh— and if this is the part where I'm supposed to get the classic alien anal probe, can I request a steady rhythm? I'm not a fan of the 'random surge' setting."

Gabriel looked away, smiling despite himself.

Voss's jaw clenched. "Your sarcastic humor is not helping."

"Oh, I'm sorry," Nathan said sweetly. "Would you rather I cry or hyperventilate? Because honestly, I can do both. At the same time."

Another pulse. Stronger.

Voss pointed sharply at the container. "Control that thing."

Nathan scoffed. "Control yours. Mine actually has manners."

Gabriel choked. Emerson turned away, biting back a laugh.

Voss inhaled sharply through her nose. "Enough. Nathan, details. What exactly is your connection to it?"

"I don't know," Nathan said honestly. "It didn't come with instructions. Or a user manual. Or a guy named Tech whose last name is Support."

"Nathan—" Gabriel warned gently.

"I'm just saying," Nathan muttered. "It could've at least beeped twice for 'hi.'"

The anomaly pulsed—longer, warmer.

Voss slammed her hand on the table. "Nathan Moffett, you are being intentionally difficult."

Nathan leaned forward, voice lowered with a sing-song imitation of happy, but with intensity. "No. I'm being intentionally sane. Because if I stop joking, I will start panicking. And if I start panicking, *that thing*—" he pointed at his container— "will probably blow up Florida."

The anomaly gave a soft, indignant pulse.

"See?" Nathan said, sitting back with exaggerated calm. "It's offended. Honestly, it probably prefers to blow up California. Nothing good ever comes out of that place."

Another pulse—sharper this time—thumped against the container wall.

Voss's eyes flashed. "You're making a mockery of this—"

Gabriel stepped between them. "Enough. He's answering you. You just don't like the delivery."

Voss spun toward Gabriel. "Oh, I know his delivery. I know yours even better."

Nathan frowned. "What is that supposed to—"

But Voss wasn't looking at him anymore. Her gaze locked on Gabriel with a cold, cutting familiarity.

"You never told him, did you?"

Gabriel's posture changed instantly. He didn't move. He didn't breathe.

Nathan's stomach dropped. "Told me… what?"

Voss didn't wait.

"You want to know who Gabriel was?" she said. "Before Disney. Before you. Before things fell from the sky?"

"Voss," Gabriel warned.

She ignored him.

"He was the one we sent on missions no one else would survive…"

As Voss spoke, Nathan's heartbeat accelerated—fear mixing with confusion and betrayal. The anomaly answered *immediately* with a deeper pulse, a low hum that vibrated through the container like a tightening coil.

Nathan swallowed hard. "Gabriel…?"

Gabriel's eyes flicked downward. "Nathan—"

Voss continued, relentless. Every word hit Nathan harder. Every pulse from the anomaly grew stronger—resonant, metallic, almost protective.

Nathan swallowed. His hands trembled. The anomaly rattled violently now, pulses overlapping, climbing, matching him beat for beat.

Voss stepped toward him. "You're wondering who you're dating? This is who he is—"

"Nathan," Gabriel said softly, "you don't need to listen to her—"

"WHY NOT?" Nathan snapped.

The spike of emotion slammed through him. The anomaly *ignited* in response—a light ripping through its containment seams in a violent flare.

Gabriel jerked his gaze to the anomaly. Reaching for him,

"Nathan—calm down—"

"Do not touch me," Nathan whispered. It was not to Gabriel, but it sounded like it. He spoke to the room itself. To the thing reacting to him. Not anger—fear. Fear of what the anomaly might unleash if he spiraled further.

The anomaly pulsed again—heavy, frantic, mirrors of his heart pounding in his chest.

"Nathan—" Gabriel tried again, softer. "Breathe. Please. Just—"

But Nathan couldn't. His heartbeat was a roar. His vision tunneled. The anomaly pulsed harder and harder—outward like a stormfront – not attacking, but trying to reach him.

And then— Everything stilled.

A presence brushed his mind. Soft. Warm. Familiar.

Not words. Not speech.

Just: I'm here.

Nathan gasped and stumbled back hard against the seat.

His anomaly pulsed in sync.

And Gabriel flinched— because he felt it too.

A second voice. In his own mind.

Nathan's voice. Panicked. Hurting.

Gabriel?

Gabriel inhaled sharply. *Nathan.*

"Oh hell," Emerson whispered, staring at his scanner. "Commander—this is new."

Voss snapped around. "What?"

Emerson held up the device, showing two synchronized waveform patterns.

"They're communicating telepathically," Emerson said. "Through the anomalies."

Voss blinked. "You're telling me—"

"Yes," Emerson said. "They're linked."

Nathan stared at Gabriel, trembling.

Gabriel took a slow breath.

"Nathan," he said aloud and across their new connection, "I'm right here."

"Gabriel, is what she said real about you?" Nathan spoke telepathically. "Some," came his reply, "They did lose me, but you and I found each other."

The anomalies pulsed together—warm, bright, protective.

Voss's face went pale.

Because nothing in their training—nothing in their protocols—prepared them for a bonded pair of humans emotionally tethered through alien technology.

And certainly not these two.

Not Gabriel and Nathan. Not *them*.

(8) RESTRAINTS

The interrogation room emptied one pair of boots at a time.

Each retreating step echoed off the bare concrete walls—deliberate, measured, the sound of people who had already decided Nathan was no longer worth watching. One by one, they filed out until only Commander Voss remained. She stood with arms folded tight across her chest, jaw set like polished steel under the single overhead light. The bulb hummed faintly, a low electronic drone that drilled into Nathan's temples almost as aggressively as her stare.

"You think sarcasm helps you?" she asked. Her voice was flat, professional, the kind of calm that promised consequences.

"Oh absolutely," Nathan muttered, throat still raw from earlier shouting. "Especially when dealing with people who cut their hair with a—"

He didn't get to finish.

A sharp, cold sting bloomed at the side of his neck—precise, immediate, paralyzing. The sensation raced outward like ice cracking through veins. He gasped, hand jerking up on instinct to swat at the source, but his fingers only brushed air before the world smeared sideways.

Two silhouettes materialized around him—security medics? Agents in tactical gear? Faces blurred into shadow. Voss didn't flinch. She simply watched, expression unchanging, as though she'd been waiting for this exact moment all along.

"Nigh—… Gabri—…" The syllables dissolved on his tongue, thick and useless.

Darkness folded over him like wet canvas—slow at first, then sudden and complete.

He woke to straps.

Thick industrial webbing—black, reinforced, smelling faintly of machine oil and neoprene—clamped across his wrists, chest, thighs, and forehead. A metal frame cradled his body at a slight incline; the surface was cold through the thin paper gown, chilling the small of his back. Overhead, fluorescent tubes buzzed faintly, their light harsh and clinical, throwing long shadows across the bare walls. The air was colder here—filtered, dry, carrying the sterile bite of antiseptic and heated metal.

But what snapped him fully into consciousness wasn't the cold, or the light, or even the ache in his limbs.

It was the absolute, bone-deep knowledge that he could not move.

Nathan's breathing spiked—short, frantic bursts that made the chest strap press harder against his ribs. Each inhale felt stolen, shallow; each exhale rattled in his throat. He jerked his arms— only an inch before the bindings bit back, leather and steel grinding against skin. Panic surged fast and choking-hot, flooding his chest until it felt like drowning on dry land.

"No—no, no-no, no-no—" The words tumbled out, cracked and high. "Let me go—HEY! LET ME—!"

He thrashed.

Hard.

The frame rattled violently—metal clanging against metal. Straps scraped raw patches on his wrists; the chest restraint tightened automatically, squeezing air from his lungs in a punishing cinch. Something overhead creaked in protest. His pulse hammered in his ears, drowning the room in white noise. He couldn't see the door from this angle—only ceiling tiles, flickering light strips, and the cold gleam of a security camera lens high in the corner, red recording light steady and unblinking.

He was trapped. Hours had passed—he could feel it in the stiffness of his joints, the sour dryness in his mouth, the faint chemical aftertaste still coating his tongue from whatever they'd injected. And they had separated him from—

Nathan.

The voice wasn't a voice.

It slid through his mind like a thought he hadn't generated—quiet, warm, unmistakable.

Nathan froze. His chest rose and fell in uneven, shuddering bursts.

"…Gabriel?" he whispered.

Yes. I'm here. Not close—but I'm here. Stay still. Stay breathing. Please.

Nathan squeezed his eyes shut. Relief crashed against confusion and terror, tangling into something he couldn't name. "Where are you?"

A pause—long enough that Nathan felt the distance between them like miles of concrete and steel.

Underground. Different facility. They're not letting me near you. Something… happened after you were sedated. I heard alarms. Someone shouted that your anomaly breached containment.

Nathan's stomach dropped through the floor. "My—what?"

The thing that came from the fountain. The ring-composite. The material that fused. It didn't stay in the containment dome. It… left. It moved on its own.

His mouth went dry, tongue sticking to the roof. "Is it coming to me?"

Yes. That's what they're afraid of.

Gabriel's presence flickered—strained, like a radio signal crossing storm fronts.

Nathan, listen. They think we're connected. They're starting to realize the first anomaly chose you. And after the second one hit...

"Wait—second—what second? What hit?"

I don't know yet. They're not telling me anything. But they're scared. And Voss... she's furious. Something about protocol being 'compromised.'

Nathan tried to lift his head; the padded neck restraint stopped him cold. A frustrated growl tore from his throat.

"Gabriel, I can't get out of these. I can't even move my damn head."

Don't struggle. It tightens the harness. They designed it to restrain non-human threats.

"Non-human—oh, perfect," Nathan snapped, voice cracking on the edge of hysteria. "So now I'm a biohazard."

You're not. They're reacting out of fear. But we need to get out. I just don't know how yet.

The connection dimmed again—static washing over Gabriel's mind like interference from distant thunder.

"Gabriel—?"

Nathan, listen. Your anomaly... it fought. I heard the blast doors seal. They couldn't stop it. If it finds you before we do—

"Before we do what?"

Before we escape. Both of us. Together.

Nathan's breath hitched—sharp, painful.

I will find you. No matter where they moved you. But you have to hold on. I can feel the anomaly searching for you. It's getting closer. And it's not… calm.

A metal clang thundered somewhere beyond the room—distant but unmistakable. The sound rolled through the walls like a slow earthquake.

Nathan's eyes widened, pupils dilating in the harsh light.

"…Gabriel?"

I heard that too.

Another clang. Closer.

This time the lights flickered—once, twice—strobing the room in sick pulses of white and shadow.

Nathan's restrained body trembled as vibrations crept up through the frame—into his spine, his teeth, his skull. A pulse. Slow. Rhythmic. Deliberate.

He knew that pattern.

He felt that pattern.

The same presence that had reached for him at the fountain in the rain-soaked plaza, that had surged through his veins in the ruined lab, that had called to him in dreams he still couldn't fully remember—

It was here. Somewhere in the facility.

And it wanted him.

"Gabriel—it's coming."

I know. I feel it too. Stay awake. Don't slip under again. I'm moving now. I'm going to find a way out of my bunker, I swear it.

The lights flickered a second time—longer, more erratic.

Then went out entirely.

Darkness crashed down, absolute and suffocating. No emergency strips, no red glow from the camera, no faint seepage under the door. Only black.

Nathan sucked in a breath—sharp, ragged.

In the pitch-dark, only the thrum remained.

Steady. Deliberate. Closer with every heartbeat.

The alien intelligence was closing the distance—floor by floor, corridor by corridor—its presence pressing against the edges of Nathan's awareness like warm stone against skin.

And in the silence between pulses, Nathan heard something else: the faint, distant screech of metal giving way.

The thing that had chosen him was coming. And nothing in this facility was going to stop it.

(9) THE THINGS THAT FIND US

Darkness swallowed the room whole.

It wasn't the clean black of a power outage; it was thick, tactile, pressing against Nathan's eyeballs like damp velvet. The air tasted stale—filtered through concrete, metal, and the faint metallic tang of recycled oxygen. Every inhale carried the faint chemical bite of whatever disinfectant they used on the restraints. The straps themselves were worse: wide leather cuffs lined with something synthetic that had warmed to body temperature, yet still felt alien against his skin. Each buckle pressed a cold crescent of steel into his wrists and ankles, biting just enough to remind him he was pinned like a specimen.

Nathan didn't move. Not because he didn't want to—every muscle screamed to thrash—but because panic had locked him halfway between a breath and a scream. His heart hammered so hard he could feel it in his teeth.

And beneath all of that—

The thrum.

Faint. Steady. Deliberate.

It lived in the marrow of his bones rather than in his ears. A low-frequency vibration that made the fillings in his molars ache and his scalp prickle as though invisible fingers were brushing the fine hairs at his nape. It wasn't loud. It wasn't violent. It was worse.

It was familiar.

Nathan.

Gabriel's voice sliced through the dark like a thin wire of warmth—sharp, urgent, threading directly into the space behind Nathan's eyes.

"I'm here," Nathan whispered. His own voice sounded small, swallowed by the room.

It's in your wing. I can feel its movement. It's— The connection crackled, warped like static dragged across wet glass. *—not hostile. Not yet. But it's in distress.*

"Distress?" Nathan hissed through clenched teeth. "Pretty sure *I'm* the one strapped to a bed."

It's coming to you because it thinks you're hurt. Or threatened. Or both.

Nathan's pulse stuttered. The idea that something so vast, so inhuman, could sense the sour copper taste of his fear in the air made nausea roll through him in slow, greasy waves. Sweat prickled along his hairline, then slid cold down his temple.

"Gabriel, you need to get here."

I'm trying. But my bunker isn't fully sealed. More like... poorly supervised. A ragged breath ghosted through the link. *I think they underestimated how much being near the anomalies changed me.*

Nathan blinked uselessly into the black. "Changed you how?"

Before Gabriel could answer, metal screamed somewhere beyond the door.

Not like a hinge turning. Not like a tool scraping. Like pressure peeling steel back layer by layer—slow, deliberate, almost careful.

The sound vibrated up through the bed frame, into Nathan's spine. He felt it in his ribs.

Gabriel's voice sharpened. *It's right outside your sector. Nathan, listen to me—do NOT show fear. It responds to emotional flux. Stay as calm as possible.*

"Oh yeah," Nathan muttered, throat so dry the words rasped. "Because that's easy."

Nathan—

Another metallic shriek cut him off.

This one was right at the door.

Nathan's breath hitched. The restraints creaked with each shallow inhale; the thin mattress beneath him trembled in sympathy. He could feel the anomaly now—its presence pressing against the edges of the room like the air itself was being displaced, thickened, pushed aside to make room for something immense and unseen. The temperature dropped a sudden five degrees; gooseflesh raced up his arms beneath the thin hospital gown.

Then—

CLANG.

Not a knock. A test.

The anomaly was feeling for structural weakness—probing the door like a tongue testing a loose tooth.

"Gabriel—"

I'm coming. Hold on. I've almost reached the auxiliary stairwell. But Nathan—if it gets to you before I do, don't panic. It doesn't want to hurt you. It wants to reconnect. It thinks you're part of it.

"Fantastic," Nathan breathed. His voice cracked on the last syllable.

The door bolt groaned—long and low, metal fibers protesting as something immense leaned into them.

Then something heavier dragged itself down the outer frame—slow, deliberate, leaving deep grooves that Nathan could *hear*: a fingernails-on-chalkboard screech drawn out into minutes. The vibration traveled through the floor, up the bed legs, into his skeleton.

CLANG. Harder. More intentional.

The overhead lights flickered back on for half a second—harsh fluorescent white that burned afterimages into his retinas—then died again.

In that stolen flash, Nathan saw it: a ripple of sand-like particulate pouring under the door seam. Not ordinary sand. Grains of fused stone—black, glassy, glinting with inner heat—like volcanic ash that remembered being magma.

The grains gathered, quivering, then pulled upward. They rose in slow, liquid spirals, reforming like mercury poured in reverse—building a column that thickened, tightened, shaped itself into something almost humanoid, though the edges kept sloughing and re-forming.

A low hum filled the room.

The same pitch he'd heard at the fountain. In the lab. In the dreams that left him waking with salt on his lips.

The door latch popped with a soft, final *snick*.

The door swung open without a sound—no hinges squealing, no draft following.

No creature stood in the frame.

Just that shifting column of particulate matter—forming, collapsing, reforming—as though it were auditioning shapes, searching for the one that would feel right.

And then it sensed him.

The entire mass pivoted toward the bed like iron filings aligning to a magnet. The hum deepened—became a resonance that sank into Nathan's chest and wrapped around his heart. His skin prickled violently; every hair stood at attention. The air around the entity shimmered with heat distortion, carrying the faint mineral scent of hot stone and ozone.

The particles tightened into spirals, threads, delicate looping tendrils that reached forward—almost like—

Hands.

Reaching.

The straps on Nathan's wrists trembled—not from his shaking, but from the anomaly's proximity. Micro-vibrations traveled through the leather, through his skin.

It was trying to free him.

"Gabriel—"

I see it. I'm at the observation glass. Nathan—I'm here. I'm looking right at you.

Nathan jerked his head to the side.

There—beyond the reinforced window across the containment hall—Gabriel stood, palms flat to the glass, breath fogging the surface in rapid, panicked bursts. His eyes were wide, pupils blown, face pale under the emergency lighting.

For one suspended heartbeat, Nathan forgot the terror and locked eyes with him.

"Gabriel," he whispered, "help me."

"I'm trying. I just need—"

Behind Gabriel, security alarms detonated—shrill, overlapping klaxons that drilled into Nathan's skull. Red emergency lights pulsed. Armed agents sprinted down the corridor toward him, boots pounding concrete.

Nathan's heart plummeted. "No—Gabriel—GO!"

Gabriel didn't run.

Instead, he pressed his forehead to the glass, voice breaking through the psychic link like shattered crystal: *Nathan, I won't leave you. Not again. Not this time.*

The anomaly reacted to Gabriel's raw emotion like a match to dry tinder. Its hum spiked—pure, piercing resonance—shaking every metal fixture in the room. Light fixtures rattled. The bed frame sang like a struck tuning fork.

SCH-CHOOOOM—

The straps across Nathan's chest snapped with whip-crack reports. The ones on his arms split. The ankle restraints tore. The bed frame buckled inward with a tortured groan.

Nathan gasped—air rushing into lungs that had forgotten how to expand. He sat upright for the first time in hours—free, but trembling so violently his teeth chattered. The anomaly surged forward like a breaking wave of living stone.

Agents shouted orders. Gabriel shouted louder—voice hoarse, desperate.

And for the first time, Nathan shouted back at something he barely understood:

"STOP!"

Everything froze.

The anomaly hovered inches from his face—still, waiting, listening. Particles hung suspended in mid-spiral; the hum dropped to a soft, expectant throb.

It had been waiting for that exact command.

The room held its breath with him.

61

(10) THE SHIELD AND THE SIGNAL

For several long seconds after the gunfire died away, the world shrank to the interior of the shimmering dome around Nathan. An iridescent sphere, translucent yet solid, hummed with a soft, resonant intelligence that vibrated through his bones. He floated in its center—suspended, held, encircled—by something alive but gentle. It didn't smother or restrain; it simply *protected*, like a hand cupped around a fragile flame.

For the first time since waking strapped to that cold metal bed, Nathan felt something other than raw terror. A quiet spark. A strange, tentative reassurance blooming in his chest.

The seam in the shield parted like liquid light, allowing Gabriel to slip through. It sealed instantly behind him—molten threads reweaving in perfect symmetry, zipper-fast and silent. Gabriel's breath came in sharp bursts; his eyes darted wildly between Nathan and the glowing wall, weapon still half-raised, knuckles white.

"Nathan—are you hurt? Did it—"

Nathan lifted a hand, palm out. "Relax," he said quietly. His own voice surprised him—steady, almost calm. "It's not hurting me. I promise."

Gabriel froze mid-step. "How do you *know* that?"

Nathan turned toward the inner surface and pressed his palm flat against it. The anomaly answered immediately.

Light rippled outward from the point of contact in slow, concentric waves. The shield's color shifted—deepening to a rich amber glow, warm as hearth fire. Within the hexagonal lattice, shapes began to swirl: faint symbols, fractured geometries, fleeting fragments of images that refused to hold still.

And then the barrier pulsed.

Nathan's vision fractured—not painfully, but like looking through a thousand layered panes of glass. The room dissolved into translucent overlays, each revealing glimpses of something vast, timeless, wordless.

Not memories. Not dreams. *Instructions.* A sequence—broken, incomplete, but urgent.

Gabriel rushed forward, boots scraping concrete. "Nathan— Nathan, talk to me—what's happening?"

Nathan shook his head slowly, eyes half-lidded, tracking movements no one else could see. "Give me a second. I'm… being shown something."

"Shown *what?*"

"I don't know yet." He squinted, leaning closer to the inner wall as though the images might clarify if he stared hard enough. "I'm trying to piece these clues together, but without any Scooby snacks, it's a bit more difficult."

Gabriel blinked. "…Scooby snacks?"

"Metaphorical problem-solving carbs, Gabriel. Keep up."

The anomaly pulsed—actually *approving.* Nathan felt it ripple through him like quiet laughter. And in that approval, the visions sharpened, coming into cruel focus:

Two entities streaking down through the upper atmosphere like molten stone meteors—one slightly larger, steady and resonant; the other smaller, vibrating at a higher, almost frantic pitch. Their descent fractured mid-entry: a sudden branching of trajectories. The larger one arced toward the surface near an old fountain—

calm, curious, stabilizing—drawn inexorably to Nathan like iron to a magnet. The smaller plunged deeper, faster, striking harder—drawn not to peace but to something raw and unresolved.

Drawn to Gabriel.

Nathan staggered, catching himself against the shield. "It... it wasn't random."

Gabriel stiffened, weapon lowering an inch. "What wasn't?"

"These two anomalies—they're connected. Bonded. They're supposed to function as a matched pair. A... relational unit, I guess." Nathan swallowed hard, throat dry. "And they want what we have."

"What we—" Gabriel's voice cracked on the word. "Nathan— why? Why *us*?"

"Because we're bonded too." The realization hit Nathan like cold water; he looked up, meeting Gabriel's wide eyes. "They're mimicking us."

Gabriel took an involuntary step back—but the anomaly pulsed again, soft confirmation washing over them both.

"There's more," Nathan continued, gaze returning to the swirling lattice. "The second anomaly—the one coming for us—should be stable. It's supposed to complement this one." He tapped the shield lightly. "But it's not calm. It's unstable because—"

He hesitated, the words sticking.

Gabriel's voice dropped to a whisper. "Because of me."

The shield flickered—once, uncertain.

Nathan turned fully toward him. "Gabriel... It's not blaming you. It's just reacting to everything inside you that you haven't faced.

The grief. The guilt. The things you keep locked down so tight they've become weapons."

A deep rumble tore through the facility—closer now. The second anomaly's roar vibrated the walls; dust sifted from ceiling tiles like slow gray snow. The floor trembled under their feet.

Gabriel flinched, shoulders hunching—but Nathan felt the anomaly respond differently this time. Not to fear, but to something softer.

Sympathy.

The shield brightened, its glow reaching tentatively toward Gabriel—acknowledging him, recognizing the invisible thread that tethered him to its frantic counterpart.

Nathan drew a slow, deliberate breath. "Gabriel… I think part of this is mine to solve, but part of it is yours, too. The visions—these clues—they're not just instructions for me. They're for both of us. It's teaching me how to stabilize your anomaly *through* you."

"How?" Gabriel's voice shook, raw. "Nathan, that thing coming here—it doesn't feel like it wants to be stabilized. It feels like it wants to tear the building apart to get to me."

"Because it's desperate." Nathan stepped closer. "It wants *you.* And it's terrified of losing the connection. That's why it's raging. That's why it's breaking everything in its path."

Gabriel stared at the shield, expression shifting—fear giving way, slowly, to something like recognition. Like looking at a mirror, he hadn't realized was there.

Nathan reached out and gently gripped Gabriel's wrist, thumb pressing over the pulse point. "You didn't damage it, Gabriel. It's bonded to you. And right now, that bond is the only thing keeping it from going full Godzilla."

Despite everything—the shaking walls, the approaching roar—Gabriel huffed a weak, stunned laugh. "Godzilla? Really?"

"You're welcome," Nathan said, a small smile tugging at his mouth. "That's another metaphorical Scooby snack."

The anomaly pulsed again—warm, approving, almost fond.

Then the shield flickered once more—twice—before projecting a new sequence of symbols across the inner surface. Nathan's mind snapped into sudden, crystalline focus.

"Oh," he whispered. "I think I know what to do."

The facility convulsed violently as the second anomaly reached the outer bulkhead. Metal screamed; concrete cracked. The first anomaly tightened its dome around them, folding luminous layers inward like a protective serpent coiling tighter.

Gabriel looked at Nathan—fear still there, but now threaded with a fragile spark of faith.

"Tell me."

Nathan tightened his grip on Gabriel's hand, fingers interlocking.

"We're going to help them reunite," he said softly. "And we're going to do it together."

The anomaly glowed brighter—resonating in deep, harmonious agreement—as the second anomaly finally cracked through the final barrier, its wild energy howling just beyond the shield's edge.

(11) THE MEMORY OF HUNGER

The second anomaly struck the bulkhead like a living earthquake.

Dust sifted from the ceiling in slow, gray curtains. Overhead pipes shrieked in protest, metal groaning as though something immense were twisting it from the inside. The floor beneath Nathan's boots rippled—concrete briefly liquefying into waves that lapped at his ankles before snapping back solid. He staggered, knees buckling, but Gabriel was already there: one arm hooking around Nathan's waist, the other bracing against the wall as the aftershock rolled through them both like thunder trapped in bone.

The first anomaly responded instantly. Its protective corridor tightened—hexagonal cells snapping together with soft metallic clicks, the faint ember-glow flaring to blazing amber. Light pulsed along the seams, warm yet fierce, like a heartbeat trying to outrun panic.

Gabriel's grip tightened. "Nathan—what did you see? You said you knew what to do."

Nathan blinked hard against the afterimages still fracturing at the corners of his vision: jagged shards of stained glass, colors too vivid, edges too sharp. They refused to settle into coherent memory.

"It showed me," he whispered, voice raw. "How they arrived. How they tore apart. And… why they're scared."

Gabriel's jaw worked. "Why *we're* scared," he corrected quietly.

Another impact. Closer. Sharper. The wall beside them buckled inward a fraction, hairline fractures racing across the surface like lightning in reverse. The air tasted metallic—ozone and rust and something sweeter, almost floral, like burning memory.

"Gabriel, your anomaly…" Nathan's words caught. "It's terrified it's going to lose you."

Gabriel swallowed, Adam's apple bobbing. His eyes flicked to the glowing corridor walls, then back to Nathan. "And yours—"

"Mine wants your anomaly to feel whole again," Nathan finished. The words felt too big, too intimate, like confessing something sacred in a collapsing tomb.

The shield pulsed—almost a nod. On the far side of the wall, the second anomaly shrieked: a sound like steel grief being bent into new shapes, mourning and rage braided together.

Nathan grabbed Gabriel's forearm, fingers digging in. "We need to get out of here. Before these two reunite in the middle of a bunker that was never built to survive the divine couple's therapy session."

Gabriel huffed—a short, shaky laugh that didn't reach his eyes. "Right. Escape now. Break the cosmic marriage counseling loop later."

The anomaly rippled in what could only be amusement: a soft shimmer along the hexagonal cells, like sunlight on water. But then—something shifted. The glow softened from combat amber to a warmer, almost domestic gold. Nathan felt it nudge inside his ribcage, gentle but insistent.

A need.

Not its need.

Theirs.

Food. Water. Warmth. Rest. The simple, animal requirements of flesh and blood. The anomaly understood them—not as abstract data, but as something precious it had once known.

"Nathan…" Gabriel's voice dropped, watchful. "Is it… reading you?"

Nathan shook his head slowly. "Not reading. *Caring.* It doesn't want us to collapse while we escape."

As if in proof, a slender tendril of shimmering mineral extruded from the wall—cautious, almost tentative. It curled around a fallen emergency ration pack that had skittered across the floor during the quake, lifted it delicately, and placed it at Nathan's boots. A second tendril retrieved a cracked canteen, water sloshing inside, and set it beside Gabriel.

Nathan's throat closed. "It remembers something."

The vision came then—not violent, not shattering. Gentle. Welcoming. He didn't fight it; he let it wash over him like a warm tide.

The shield dissolved for a heartbeat into an image:

Two entities drifting through a starless void—twin comets trailing faint luminous wakes. The smaller one pulsed steadily, warm orange-gold, extending filaments of energy toward the larger, dimmer form whenever it faltered. Shared sustenance. A slow transfer of resonance, heat, and coherence. Not food in any human sense, but closeness made tangible: one sustaining the other through endless night. A ritual of mutual survival. A marriage written in radiation and silence.

Nathan surfaced from the vision with tears prickling his eyes. "They… used to share meals. Not food—but energy. Warmth. Like a ritual of being-together. When one weakened, the other poured itself in until balance returned."

Gabriel watched him, expression unreadable but soft at the edges. "And now it wants us to… replicate that?"

"Not exactly." Nathan bit the inside of his cheek, tasting copper. "It wants to comfort its counterpart. And it thinks—" He hesitated, heat rising in his face. "It thinks our bond will help calm the second anomaly when they finally reunite."

"Our bond," Gabriel echoed. The word hung between them, fragile and heavy.

Nathan turned to face him fully. His chest ached with everything he hadn't said for weeks—months, maybe. "Gabriel… I need you. Not just to survive this. I need *you*. And I think it feels that. It needs to see us… connected. Resolute. Together."

Before Gabriel could answer, the corridor shuddered again. The second anomaly slammed through another layer of concrete; its energy signature whirled beyond the wall like a black sun devouring light.

Nathan stumbled forward—straight into Gabriel's arms. Gabriel caught him, arms closing instinctively, strong and steady.

FWUUUUMPH.

The shield expanded in luminous folds, wrapping them both in a protective cocoon. The air inside thickened, turned soft and warm, resonant with an ancient affection that hummed against their skin. It smelled faintly of sun-warmed stone and distant rain.

Gabriel froze, breath catching against Nathan's hair. "Nathan… what's happening?"

Nathan pressed a palm to Gabriel's sternum, feeling the frantic thud of his heart slow under the touch. "It's remembering. And… it likes us together. It wants to stabilize its mate through us— through what we feel."

The anomaly hummed—a low, rhythmic vibration that sank into their bones, easing the knots in Nathan's spine, quieting the tremor in Gabriel's hands. Nathan leaned his forehead against Gabriel's shoulder, closing his eyes.

"Don't pull away."

"I'm not," Gabriel whispered, voice rough. "I'm right here."

The cocoon tightened—softly, protectively—like arms enfolding them both. Nathan felt the anomaly's quiet joy ripple through the space: a harmonic chord forming in the air, sweet and aching.

Outside, the second anomaly's screaming energy shifted—less frantic, more searching. A question instead of a demand.

Nathan pulled back just enough to meet Gabriel's eyes. They were very close; he could see the faint freckles across Gabriel's nose, the way his pupils had dilated in the golden light.

"We have to move," Nathan said softly. "But not like this. Together. Through the sublevels. There's a vented access shaft—the anomaly showed me in the vision. It's narrow, but stable. It'll take us toward the surface access points."

Gabriel nodded, still holding him. One hand slid to the small of Nathan's back, steadying. "Lead the way."

Nathan squeezed Gabriel's hand. The anomaly responded immediately: the cocoon unfolded with graceful deliberation, reforming into a luminous corridor that stretched deeper into the dark. Tendrils of light traced the path ahead, gentle beacons.

For the first time since the anomalies had torn open the world, Nathan wasn't afraid.

Not of the things that lived beyond physics.

Not of the visions that carved themselves into his mind.

Not even of the darkness waiting below.

Because Gabriel was here—solid, warm, breathing—and now both anomalies wanted them reunited, alive, whole.

Together.

The corridor pulsed once, encouraging, and they stepped forward into it side by side.

(12) WHAT WAS BROKEN

The access corridor narrowed into a steep metal throat, its grated floor echoing under their footsteps. The anomaly's protective corridor glided with them like a living lantern, illuminating the rusted walls and abandoned equipment strewn across the lower level.

Far above, faint booms from the second anomaly rattled the pipes.

Nathan squeezed Gabriel's hand tighter. "Don't let go."

"I won't," Gabriel whispered. He sounded steady, but the tremor beneath his words betrayed something heavier — something waiting to open.

The anomaly felt it too.

The protective corridor pulsed in a slow, questioning rhythm. Your tether is frayed. Your resonance is incomplete. Why?

Nathan blinked. "Gabriel… it wants to know why your connection to your anomaly is unstable."

Gabriel exhaled and leaned against the wall, running a hand through his hair. His eyes were darker than the corridor. Tired. Haunted.

"I figured it would ask eventually."

Nathan stepped closer, touching Gabriel's arm. "You don't have to—"

Gabriel cut him off gently. "I do. It won't stabilize unless I do."

The anomaly dimmed to a low, warm glow — a quiet encouragement.

Gabriel swallowed. And then: "I have a son."

Nathan froze.

Gabriel's voice cracked — not from fear, but from the weight of carrying this alone for too long.

"His name is Tyler. He's ten."

Nathan's breath hitched. "Ten… Gabriel, that's—"

"I know." Gabriel closed his eyes. "I was a kid myself when I became a father. Twenty-one. Terrified. Barely holding my own life together."

The anomaly hummed, images forming in the air — an echo of Gabriel's emotional frequency, showing a shadow of a boy clinging to a father who kept disappearing behind obligations, missions, secrets.

Gabriel didn't look away. He continued.

"His mother and I weren't together. But I tried to be there. Every weekend. Every call. Every birthday." His voice softened into something fragile. "When the anomalies made first contact — years ago, before the public knew anything — I was recruited for early analysis."

Nathan frowned. "Years ago? Gabriel… why didn't you ever tell me that?"

"Because I wasn't allowed to. And because everything that happened after…" He swallowed hard. "It broke something in me."

The anomaly pulsed sympathetically. Nathan moved closer, gently touching Gabriel's hand.

"What happened?" he whispered.

Gabriel inhaled shakily.

"They told us the anomaly we were studying was dormant. Safe. But something woke it — something triggered a resonance spike."

A vision flashed:

—Gabriel is standing in a sealed lab —white light exploding —
a gravitational pulse tearing through the room—people falling
—Gabriel was thrown backward into reinforced glass

He looked away, shame trembling in his hands.

"I panicked. I bolted. I locked myself in a side corridor and hit
the emergency shutdown." His voice hollowed. "The anomaly
collapsed inward and… it killed two of my team."

Nathan's chest tightened. "Gabriel… you were trying to protect
yourself."

"I was trying to get home to my son," Gabriel said, voice
breaking. "That's all I was thinking. And because of that, people
died."

The anomaly thrummed — not accusing, not condemning — but
recognizing. Nathan didn't hesitate. He stepped fully into
Gabriel's space, hands on his shoulders.

"Listen to me. You didn't kill them. The situation did. The lies
your superiors told did. Fear did. You're human, Gabriel.
Terrified humans make imperfect choices."

Gabriel's eyes glistened.

"But the anomaly bonded to me that day," he whispered. "The
one we're running from right now. It was imprinted on my panic.
My grief. My guilt. That's why it's unstable. That's why it
screams when it feels me slipping toward fear."

Nathan ran a thumb along Gabriel's cheekbone. "Then we help
it rewrite that imprint."

Gabriel blinked. "Rewrite it… How?"

Nathan nodded toward the first anomaly.

"It showed me. In the visions. Anomalies don't bond through strength or control. They bond through connection. Harmony. Shared emotion."

Gabriel looked at him. "Nathan… what do we have that could stabilize something that powerful?"

Nathan lifted Gabriel's hand and pressed it to his chest.

"This," he said quietly. "Whatever this is between us."

Gabriel's lips parted in a stunned breath — but before he could respond, the corridor shook violently.

The second anomaly was close. Too close. The first anomaly surged forward, forming a shield around both men — and for the first time, the shield extended a filament of its light outward, reaching blindly through the air. Searching. Calling.

Nathan's breath caught. "It's sending out a signal. A reassurance."

Gabriel felt it too — a warm, electric thrum in his chest that mirrored the shield's frequency.

"It wants to show my anomaly that I'm not afraid," he whispered.

Nathan held him tighter. "Then don't be. I've got you. And wherever Tyler is, together, we've got him."

The corridor lights flickered, buzzing like anxious insects.

Then — silently, impossibly — the second anomaly emerged from the darkness beyond the next archway.

A towering storm of fragments, swirling black-metallic and violent with grief. Nathan braced. Gabriel went still. The first anomaly brightened. The second anomaly roared. And then— Gabriel reached out a trembling hand.

"I'm not running this time."

The roar died instantly — collapsing into a confused, trembling hum.

Nathan felt something then — something vast and emotional — through the anomalies' resonance:

Loneliness. Loss. Fear of abandonment. And a longing —a longing for reunion, like the ache of a missing limb.

The first anomaly floated forward. The second anomaly moved closer. And slowly, cautiously, the two entities' particles began to align — orbiting each other's frequency like lovers rediscovering a forgotten dance.

Nathan didn't dare breathe. Gabriel stepped closer, voice soft, cracked but steady:

"You're not alone anymore."

The anomalies pulsed — in harmony this time.

Nathan's vision flooded again, but this time it didn't hurt. This time it was clear — a doorway, a shaft leading up, an emergency maintenance tunnel that could get them out.

He gasped. "Gabriel, I know how we escape."

Gabriel took his hand. The anomalies cocooned them both — protective, warm, united — as the sublevel pathway shimmered into view.

And together, human and anomaly alike…began to rise.

(13) THE GIFT LEFT BEHIND

The ascent through the maintenance shaft felt like rising through a column of living starlight. The anomalies — now reunited in orbiting equilibrium — guided Nathan and Gabriel upward with a gentle pulse, like the heartbeat of a universe trying to soothe itself.

The air grew warmer as they rose. Calmer. Less fractured.

Even the walls themselves seemed to relax.

Nathan leaned into Gabriel as the cocoon of shimmering mineral light carried them upward. For the first time, the terror beneath their journey was gone. No alarms. No collapsing ceilings. No trembling ground.

Just ascent.

Just peace.

Gabriel exhaled softly. "Nathan… earlier, I didn't get to finish."

Nathan looked up. "Finish what?"

"Telling you about Tyler."

The anomalies paused their ascent — listening, learning — sensing the emotional thread. Nathan nodded. "Tell me."

A quiet smile touched Gabriel's lips. "He's ten now. Smart as hell. He looks exactly like I did at his age — same eyes, same hair, same stubborn little chin." His voice softened into a warmth Nathan had never heard before. "And he's adorable, Nathan. The kind of adorable that makes you wonder how the world ever scared him."

Nathan's heart warmed. "Gabriel… you love him so much."

"Yes." Gabriel's voice tightened, fragile with honesty. "More than I know how to say. And everything I've done — every mistake I've ever made — I carry because I was terrified of losing him."

Nathan rested his forehead against Gabriel's shoulder. "You don't have to fear that anymore. Not with me. Not with this new beginning."

The anomalies pulsed again — not intrusively, but in wonder. They absorbed the emotion. The tenderness. The depth of connection.

This was what they had struggled to understand.

Love not as possession, but as protection. Love not as fusion, but as partnership. Love not as destruction, but as creation.

The second anomaly dimmed its volatile aura. The first anomaly's glow softened.

They had learned.

As they reached the top of the shaft, the anomalies shifted, separating from Nathan and Gabriel with slow, deliberate movements, as though performing a sacred dance.

The cocoon unfolded.

A lattice of geometries blossomed in the air — shapes within shapes, light patterns orbiting like a celestial mandala. Nathan felt his breath catch as the images washed through him:

—an ancient arrival —an original purpose —a broken sequence —a longing to reunite —a misunderstanding of love —a need to control rather than harmonize

And finally:

The possibility of change.

"Nathan," Gabriel whispered, "it's showing you the core."

Nathan stepped forward instinctively, as if drawn by the inevitable. The anomaly's geometry hovered before him — a crystalline structure of unspoken code.

He lifted his hand.

His fingers brushed the light.

Instantly, his mind and heart filled with a burning brightness — not pain, but clarity. Every symbol, every broken directive, every flawed logic path flowed through him like music waiting for its final chord.

Nathan whispered, "Love doesn't need to consume. It doesn't need to break worlds… or people… to be whole."

Gabriel gently placed his palm against Nathan's back. "I'm right here."

The anomalies thrummed — resonant, trembling — and Nathan reached into the code. He rewrote it gently. Carefully. With compassion, not force.

He didn't erase their longing. He reshaped it.

Togetherness without destruction. Unity without erasure. Bond without violence. Reunion without loss.

The anomalies vibrated in swelling harmony — rising, shifting, merging into a single, brilliant form that bathed the maintenance chamber in living starlight.

And then — silence.

Perfect, peaceful silence.

The unified anomaly floated before them, settled in its new balance. It swelled once — as if taking a final breath —Then its body dissolved into spiraling fragments of color.

The fragments wrapped gently around Nathan and Gabriel:

Warm. Soft. Loving.

A farewell embrace.

The fragments sank into their skin, into their heartbeat, into their breath—

And when the light faded…

…it left something behind.

Two objects hovered in the air between them:

An amulet of deep sapphire light for Nathan. An amulet of molten silver for Gabriel.

They drifted forward with the weight of destiny.

Nathan reached out. The sapphire amulet fell into his palm.

The moment his fingers closed around it, he felt the universe pause — as if time itself had bowed.

Gabriel caught the silver amulet.

A hum of raw energy traveled up his arm.

They didn't need an explanation.

They understood.

Nathan's amulet glowed with frozen blue light. Time stalled — pockets of time. The air stopped moving. The dust hung motionless. The heartbeat of the world held still.

Nathan gasped. "I can… stop time."

"And space," Gabriel whispered. "You can reshape it. Protect. Shield people."

He looked down at his silver amulet. His body felt light — weightless — powerful.

"I can move anything," he murmured. "Lift objects...and fly!?" He smiled in astonishment. "Nathan… I think I can fly."

A tremor rippled through the chamber — not violent, not threatening.

Transformative.

The damage the anomalies had caused… healed.

The cracked walls aligned. The scorched floors cooled. The rubble vanished. The earth reknit.

The fountain — the beginning of it all — restored itself perfectly, water bubbling peacefully as if nothing had ever occurred.

Aboveground, civilians blinked in mild confusion, unaware that any disaster had ever happened.

No trauma. No fear. No memory.

Except for Nathan and Gabriel.

The chamber filled with dawn-like stillness.

Then Gabriel froze — eyes widening.

He reached into his pocket.

His fingers brushed something solid.

He pulled it out.

Nathan gasped.

It was the ring Gabriel had crafted for him. Soft metal. Gentle shimmer. Every detail Gabriel had poured into it — full of hope, apology, love. This ring had more luster and beauty to it than it had before. It was changed by the power of love.

"Nathan," Gabriel whispered, voice trembling, "I thought this was lost."

"It wasn't," Nathan replied softly. "It just wasn't time yet."

Gabriel's eyes glistened.

He dropped to one knee.

Not out of obligation. Not out of tradition.

But out of love — the kind the anomalies had finally understood.

"Nathan," Gabriel said, breath shaking, "you are the reason I survived my past. The reason I'm not running anymore. The reason I want to be a better man — for Tyler, for myself, and for you."

He lifted the ring.

"Will you marry me?"

Nathan's breath broke. His knees shook. And the amulet at his chest glowed softly — like the universe itself was holding its breath.

"Yes," he whispered, eyes shining. "Yes. Absolutely yes."

Gabriel stood with tears in his eyes, along with Nathan, who was also with a healthy stream. Gabriel pushed the ring firmly in place on Nathan's left ring finger.

They embraced — warm, desperate, joyful — And somewhere far beyond the physical world, the anomalies pulsed in faint farewell…

Witnessing the kind of love they had almost destroyed and forced everything to find completeness.

(14) MORNING IN THE NEW WORLD

Nathan woke slowly, gently, wrapped in warmth that didn't come from blankets.

Gabriel's arms were around him — loosely, tenderly — one hand at Nathan's waist, the other draped across his chest as though it had fallen there during sleep and refused to move. Their legs were tangled, the kind of soft, effortless closeness that comes only after walls have fallen and truths have been spoken.

Nathan didn't open his eyes at first. He simply breathed.

Gabriel's chest rose and fell behind him, slow and steady. A heartbeat pressed softly against his spine.

For a moment, the world — all its strangeness, all its miracles — narrowed to something simple and perfect.

Gabriel murmured sleepily, "You're awake."

"How'd you know?"

"You breathe differently when you're awake." Gabriel's nose brushed the back of Nathan's neck. "And you get warm in the shoulders. It's adorable."

Nathan smirked. "I'm adorable now? Is that where we've landed?"

Gabriel pulled him closer. "You've always been adorable. I was just too terrified to tell you."

Nathan rolled in his arms, facing him fully now. Gabriel looked breathtaking in the morning light — hair tousled, eyes soft, smile small and honest.

"Terrified?" Nathan teased. "Of me?"

Gabriel kissed his forehead. "No. Of losing you."

Nathan's throat tightened. He cupped Gabriel's cheek, thumb brushing lightly across stubble. "You're not losing me," he whispered. "Not today. Not ever."

Gabriel exhaled a slow, relieved breath — the kind that sounded like healing.

Nathan leaned closer until their foreheads touched. "You realize," he murmured, "if we keep being this sweet, we're going to melt through the sheets."

Gabriel chuckled. "Worth it."

They kissed — slow, warm, unhurried — the kind of kiss that said *we made it, we're safe, we're home.*

When they finally broke apart, Gabriel brushed a strand of hair from Nathan's face. "I love you," he said quietly.

Nathan smiled. "I've always known. But…." The thought lingered, "I love you the mostest!"

A little later, after several more lazy kisses and whispered jokes about who was snoring last night ("It was definitely you," Nathan insisted), Nathan sat up suddenly, looking Gabriel directly in the eyes.

"Okay," he announced. "Real talk."

Gabriel blinked. "Oh boy. Should I brace myself?"

"Yes," Nathan said. "Possibly grab a helmet."

Gabriel laughed. "All right. Hit me."

Nathan counted on his fingers dramatically:

"Where is your son — Tyler — living at this moment? Who is his mom? When do I get to meet him? Will he be at our wedding?

Can we bring him here and let him grow up with us? And is he as adorable as you say, or do I get to be the judge of that myself?"

Gabriel stared at him, eyebrows raised. "So… a short list today."

Nathan nodded. "I like to keep things simple."

A soft knock sounded on the doorframe. Maria — impeccably dressed, dignified as always — stepped inside with a silver breakfast tray balanced on her arm.

"Good morning, Mr. Gabriel. Mr. Nathan." She bowed her head warmly. "I hope you two slept well. Breakfast is ready."

Nathan blinked, whispering to Gabriel, "You have a maid?"

"Technically, she's a house manager," Gabriel corrected softly. "But she threatens to throw frying pans at me if I call her anything but Maria."

Maria smirked. "As you should."

She set the tray on the small table near the window overlooking the clean, restored fountain outside — the world bright and unmarred as if the anomalies had never existed.

"I'll bring the tea and fruit shortly," she added before departing.

Nathan whispered, "I love her."

"Everyone loves her," Gabriel replied.

They sat at the breakfast table — still in pajamas, hair messy, newly engaged — as Maria served warm pastries, eggs, fresh fruit, and tea.

Gabriel placed his hand over Nathan's.

"All right," he said. "Your questions."

Nathan leaned in, eager.

Gabriel began gently.

"Tyler lives with his mom about twenty minutes from here. Her name is Claire. She's wonderful — smart, grounded, patient. We were never together romantically, but we've always been close friends." He paused, choosing his words carefully. "Claire wanted to be a mother. I wanted to be a father. And we trusted each other more than anyone else. So we decided to do it intentionally — no relationship expectations, no confusion. Just… a planned pregnancy. Medical, safe, mutual. Tyler was wanted by both of us from the very beginning."

Nathan's eyes softened. That made sense. It sounded exactly like Gabriel.

Gabriel continued, smiling softly. "She and I co-parent really well. Tyler gets the best of both of us."

Nathan's chest swelled with warmth. "When do I get to meet him?"

Gabriel didn't hesitate. "Soon. As soon as you want to."

"And the wedding?" Nathan asked.

Gabriel squeezed his hand. "He'll be at the wedding. Front row. Probably holding the rings."

Nathan's eyes misted. "And… can he come live with us?"

Gabriel's smile deepened — warm, touched, grateful.

"I would love that," he said softly. "And Claire would too, if we do it gently and give Tyler time. But yes. He can grow up with us. If you're ready for that."

Nathan pressed a hand over his heart dramatically. "Gabriel, I'm ready for anything with you. Even a mini-you running around asking why Daddy and Papa are kissing in the kitchen."

Gabriel choked on his tea. "P—Papa?"

Nathan smirked. "That's right. I said Papa. And you love it."

Gabriel covered his face with both hands. "Oh God."

Nathan leaned over and kissed his temple. "You love it," he repeated.

After a moment, Gabriel nodded into his hands. "Yes. I love it."

Nathan's heart swelled.

They sat there — talking, eating, planning — the morning sunlight spilling warm gold through the windows, the fountain bubbling peacefully outside, the world calm and untouched.

No danger. No anomalies. No chaos.

Just two men in love, building the first day of the rest of their lives.

Nathan looked at Gabriel. Gabriel looked at him. And they knew:

Life wasn't returning to normal. It was beginning.

(15) MEETING TYLER

Nathan had never been more aware of his hands.

Why were they sweaty? Why were they cold? Why did they suddenly feel like they were made of ten thumbs? He kept wiping them on his jeans, then smoothing the fabric, then lacing his fingers together — none of it helping.

Gabriel glanced over from the driver's seat of the sleek black SUV.

"You're going to wear a hole in those pants," he teased gently.

Nathan stared straight ahead, stiff as a telephone pole. "Gabriel. I am about to meet your ten-year-old son. Who looks like a miniature you. Who will definitely judge me harder than any government agency on Earth?"

Gabriel laughed softly. "Tyler is not going to interrogate you."

"Are you sure? Because he might. Kids have no filters."

"That's true," Gabriel admitted. "But he's sweet. And thoughtful. And he's excited to meet you."

Nathan froze. "He… he knows about me?"

Gabriel nodded. "I told Claire everything. And we told Tyler this morning that someone very special is going to be in his life now."

Nathan's heart thumped against his ribs. "Did you tell him about… the wedding?"

"No," Gabriel said softly. "I thought we'd save that part. Together."

A warm flutter spread through Nathan's chest. Together. That word meant everything now.

The SUV pulled up to a cozy, two-story house with a neatly trimmed lawn and a bright blue door. Sunlight poured across the porch, warming the welcome mat that read *Come as you are.*

Nathan swallowed hard.

Gabriel turned off the engine, then took Nathan's hands gently in his own.

"Nathan," he murmured, "you don't have to be perfect today. Just breathe. I love you, and Tyler will love you too. We're a family."

Nathan exhaled — or tried to. It came out as a shaky, squeaky half-breath he pretended was intentional.

"Not perfect? Pssshhhh, okay, sure, yeah—whatever." He straightened his shirt. Then his hair. Then his shirt again. "Wwwhhewww. Yep. Totally fine. I can do this."

He could not. He absolutely could not. His stomach was performing Olympic gymnastics.

But he was going to try.

Gabriel kissed his cheek — a grounding thing, warm and steady — and together they walked up to the porch.

Gabriel knocked.

Footsteps. A shifting shadow.

Nathan's spine went ramrod straight, smile locked in place, hands suddenly unsure of what to do with themselves.

The door swung open.

A woman with warm eyes, curly chestnut hair pulled into a loose bun, and the air of someone who had life under control smiled in greeting.

"Gabriel," Claire said warmly. "You look good." Then she turned to Nathan with a bright, friendly curiosity. "And you must be Nathan."

Nathan froze. "I—I am. That's me. Nathan. I'm Nathan."

Claire smiled wider. "That's a lot of Nathans, but I'll take it."

Gabriel cupped his mouth and buried a laugh.

Claire opened the door wide. "Come on in. Tyler's in the living room. He's been bouncing off the walls for twenty minutes."

The words hit Nathan like a wave. Bouncing. Excited.

Oh God.

Nathan stepped inside.

The living room was colorful and lived-in — board games stacked on shelves, a large map of the world pinned to the wall, LEGO structures mid-build on the coffee table. It smelled faintly of cinnamon and pine.

And then—

A small boy peeked over the back of the couch.

Dark hair. Bright eyes. Gabriel's exact expression when he's trying not to smile.

Tyler.

When he realized they saw him, he jumped to his feet, standing straight like he'd practiced what to do.

"Hi!" he said loudly. "I'm Tyler. You're Nathan."

Nathan blinked. "Yes. Yes, I am. Wow, you're Tyler? So handsome, just like your Dad."

Gabriel whispered, "Nice compliment."

Tyler hopped over the couch and walked right up to Nathan — stopping about two feet away. He looked him up and down, eyes wide, studying every inch.

Nathan swallowed hard. "Uh… hi."

Tyler tilted his head. Then he asked:

"Do you like dinosaurs?"

Nathan blinked. "Do… I like dinosaurs?"

Tyler nodded. "People who don't like dinosaurs can't be trusted."

Nathan leaned down slightly, matching his serious tone. "Well. Good news. I LOVE dinosaurs. Except for velociraptors. Those jerks are cheaters."

Tyler gasped. "That's EXACTLY what I say!"

Gabriel's eyes softened — the kind of soft that hinted at relief and pride and love all blended together.

Tyler reached out and grabbed Nathan's hand without hesitation.

"Come see my T. rex. He's huge."

Nathan's heart melted on the spot.

Gabriel leaned close and whispered into Nathan's ear: "Told you he'd like you."

Nathan whispered back, "Gabriel, I think I'm in love with your child. Adorable!"

Gabriel chuckled under his breath. "That makes two of us."

Later — after Tyler proudly introduced Nathan to every dinosaur in his collection and declared that Nathan was "way cooler than expected" — the three sat together in the living room.

Tyler perched between them, holding a stuffed raptor.

Nathan looked at Gabriel, then at Tyler, then quietly asked:

"Tyler… can I ask you something?"

Tyler nodded. "Anything."

Nathan's voice softened. "How would you feel if I… if I became part of your family?"

Tyler brightened. "Like my second dad?"

Nathan's breath caught. "If you want that."

Tyler shrugged happily. "I already decided. You're nice. And Daddy smiles differently when you're here. So yeah."

Gabriel's eyes glimmered — glassy and full. Nathan felt something inside him break open in the best way.

Tyler continued, matter-of-fact: "Are you and Daddy getting married?"

Nathan froze.

Gabriel squeezed his hand.

Nathan smiled. "Yes," he said softly. "We are."

Tyler grinned so big it nearly split his face. "Can I be in the wedding? Can I hold the rings? Can I wear a tie? Can I—"

Nathan laughed. "Yes. Yes to all of that."

Tyler threw his arms around Nathan's waist, hugging him fiercely.

Nathan hugged him back — this small, warm, wonderful human he never expected to love this quickly.

Gabriel watched them with a look that could have lit the room even without sunlight.

Nathan met Gabriel's eyes over Tyler's shoulder.

Everything was right.

Everything was beginning.

94

(16) A HOME BUILT FOR THREE

The drive back to Gabriel's house felt different from the drive there. Before, Nathan's nerves had been a tight, buzzing knot.

Now…

Now the three of them sat together in the back seat — Nathan, Gabriel, and Tyler — with Tyler leaning comfortably against Nathan's arm as if he'd always belonged there.

Tyler held Nathan's hand the way children do when they trust without hesitation, fingers curled and warm.

From across the seat, Gabriel watched them, eyes soft. He reached over, offering his hand so Nathan could lace their fingers together.

"Is this okay?" Nathan whispered to Tyler.

Tyler nodded. "It's okay. You're warm."

Nathan bit back a laugh. "That's good. I try to be warm."

Gabriel snorted. "You also try to be dramatic."

Nathan gasped. "I'll have you know, I don't *try* to be dramatic. I excel. It's a natural gift."

Tyler giggled. "Papa Nathan is funny."

Nathan froze. Gabriel froze. Even the driver seemed to inhale sharply.

Slowly… very slowly… Nathan looked at Gabriel. Gabriel looked back — eyes widening, lips parting.

"Nathan…" Gabriel whispered, "Did he just—"

"Yes," Nathan mouthed.

"Is it okay?" Tyler asked, suddenly unsure, eyes flicking between them.

Nathan turned fully toward him, heart swelling so hard it almost hurt. "Tyler," he said softly, "you can call me any name that makes you feel safe."

Tyler smiled shyly and leaned his head against Nathan's chest. "Okay… Papa Nathan."

Nathan's eyes stung. Gabriel's eyes stung. The air in the car suddenly felt too full, too meaningful.

Gabriel swallowed hard. "That's… perfect, buddy."

Tyler closed his eyes, content.

Nathan intertwined their hands tighter.

Maria greeted them at the door with a warm smile and absolutely no surprise when Tyler immediately flung himself onto the couch as if he lived there.

"Master Tyler," she said with a graceful bow, "welcome. Your room is already being prepared."

Tyler perked up. "I get a room here?"

Nathan and Gabriel exchanged looks.

Gabriel nodded. "If you want it."

Tyler immediately turned to Nathan. "Do you have a room?"

Nathan laughed, scooting closer. "Of course I do, silly. I have my own room… but sometimes I cozy up with your dad in his."

Tyler scrunched his nose. "Ew."

Then, without missing a beat, his curiosity lit up. "If I get scared, can I join either of you?"

Nathan softened. "Always."

"And which of you snores?" Tyler asked, eyes narrowing like a detective.

Nathan pointed at Gabriel instantly. "Him."

Gabriel sputtered. "I do *not* snore."

Tyler gasped. "Are you a blanket thief?"

Nathan raised a hand dramatically. "Oh, absolutely. He steals blankets like it's a competitive sport."

Gabriel crossed his arms. "I am surrounded by liars."

Tyler giggled, delighted. "Okay. Then maybe I'll sleep in my room… unless it gets scary. Then I'm coming to steal both your blankets."

"Oh yeah?" Nathan arched a brow. "Well, I'll have you know I'm also the House Pirate. And if you attempt any blanket-stealing mutiny, I'll make ye walk the plank."

Tyler gasped in delight. "Then I'm the Junior Captain Pirate! And I outrank you because I'm small and fast."

Gabriel sighed, deadpan. "Please do not encourage him, Nathan. I already live with one pirate. I don't need a fleet."

Tyler beamed. "Too late! We're a pirate crew now!"

Right on cue, Maria stepped gracefully into the living room with a folded blanket over her arm.

"Master Nathan," she said politely, "the staff would like to remind you that the plank is not covered under the cleaning policy."

Nathan blinked. "What—there's a policy about the plank?"

"There is now," Maria replied without missing a beat.

Tyler cackled with joy. Nathan collapsed onto the couch beside him, laughing until he couldn't breathe.

After Tyler had fallen asleep halfway through a dinosaur documentary, Gabriel lifted him gently and took him upstairs to the guest room — soon to be his room.

Nathan stayed on the couch, wrapped in a soft blanket Maria had placed around him earlier.

When Gabriel returned, he sat beside Nathan and immediately took his hand.

"You okay?" Gabriel asked softly.

Nathan nodded. "I think my heart has grown five sizes today."

Gabriel rested his head on Nathan's shoulder. "Mine too."

They sat quietly for a long moment — the kind of quiet that feels sacred.

Nathan finally whispered, "Gabriel… can I tell you something?"

"Anything."

"I never thought I'd have a family." His voice trembled. "I never thought anyone would want to love me like this. Let alone trust me with their child."

Gabriel lifted his head and turned Nathan's face toward him with gentle fingers.

"Nathan," he said, voice low and certain, "Tyler didn't choose you because I told him to. He chose you because you're kind. Because you're warm. Because you make people feel safe just by being yourself."

Nathan swallowed hard. "And you?"

Gabriel smiled softly.

"I chose you because you changed my world the moment you walked into it. And because… you're home."

Nathan's breath caught.

Gabriel leaned in and kissed him — a slow, grounding kiss, tender enough to undo him completely.

"Relax and breathe," Gabriel murmured against his lips. "I love you. Tyler will love you. We're a family."

Nathan pressed his forehead to Gabriel's.

"We're a family."

A little while later, they sat cross-legged on the living room rug, a notebook between them.

"Wedding?" Gabriel asked with a raised eyebrow.

Nathan nodded. "Wedding."

"Big or small?"

"Small," Nathan said. "But meaningful. And beautiful. And emotional enough that Maria will pretend she isn't crying."

Gabriel laughed. "She'll deny it with her last breath."

"Tyler should be the ring bearer," Nathan added.

"He claimed it earlier without hesitation," Gabriel said proudly.

Nathan hesitated for a beat, fingers brushing the edge of the notebook. "There's… something else I want to do," he said softly. "I want to gift Tyler a ring too."

Gabriel's head lifted, interest sparking in his eyes. "Oh, really? And what kind of ring would this be?"

Nathan's smile warmed with quiet conviction. "A promise ring," he said. "One that says we promise to always love him, support him, protect him… to walk with him through his growing-up years. I'm marrying into a family — *your* family — and that means being his protector and father just as much as it means being your husband."

Gabriel's breath caught. His eyes softened with something deep and grateful — almost reverent. "Nathan…" he whispered, the rest of the thought collapsing into silence as his voice threatened to break.

Nathan squeezed his hands gently. "He deserves to know he's not just welcome with us… He's chosen. For life."

Gabriel leaned forward, resting his forehead against Nathan's. "You have no idea what that means to me."

Nathan's smile warmed the space between them. "Then let's show him."

Gabriel drew back just enough to look at him fully.

"With you," he murmured, "every version of the future feels right."

Nathan smiled through the swell of emotion tightening his chest. "Then let's build it."

And together — under the soft glow of the living room lights, with Tyler sleeping upstairs and the world finally quiet — they began planning the rest of their lives.

(17) FIRST LIGHT OF A NEW FAMILY

Tyler's first night in the house felt like watching a little piece of the world finally click into place.

The whole next day had been one long, golden stretch of "right."

They played outside until the sun warmed their shoulders — throwing a baseball back and forth, Tyler shrieking with victory every time he actually caught it. Gabriel tried to teach him basketball, which lasted approximately four seconds before Tyler declared the hoop was "too tall and unfair," prompting Nathan to demand an official height inspection.

Lunch turned into a picnic on the grass, complete with juice boxes, strawberries, and Gabriel pretending not to be competitive about who could build the tallest sandwich.

Later, they all went swimming — Tyler jumping into the pool with fearless enthusiasm, clinging to Nathan's shoulders, then demanding Gabriel judge their splash sizes like it was the Olympics. Afterward came cartoons, a few favorite shows, and Tyler sprawled across both their laps like a pet does when claiming as if he owned them.

By evening, Tyler had yawned himself into a soft, wiggly puddle, insisting he wasn't tired even as his head drifted onto Nathan's arm.

After brushing his teeth (with far too much toothpaste) and insisting that raptors would definitely have been house pets if they didn't eat everything, Nathan helped tuck him into the freshly made bed Maria had prepared.

Tyler curled beneath the soft blue blankets, eyes sleepy, arms wrapped around his stuffed raptor.

Nathan adjusted the pillow. "You warm enough?"

Tyler nodded. "Are you and Daddy going to be downstairs?"

"We'll be right here. And if you need anything, call out."

Tyler's eyes fluttered. "Okay… Papa Nathan."

Nathan's heart wobbled like a loose hinge.

He leaned down and kissed Tyler's forehead. "Goodnight, kiddo."

Gabriel stood in the doorway, arms folded, wearing the softest smile Nathan had ever seen on him.

As they stepped out, Gabriel slipped his hand into Nathan's, squeezing gently.

"You handled that perfectly."

Nathan whispered, "I'm trying."

"You don't need to try. You're doing it."

The next morning, sunlight spilled into the house like it had been waiting for them.

Tyler thundered down the stairs — still in dinosaur pajamas — and launched himself onto the couch between them.

"Papa Nathan! Daddy!"

He was breathless with excitement. "There are PANCAKES in the kitchen!"

Nathan sat up dramatically. "Pancakes?! Who did this magnificent thing?"

Maria cleared her throat from the dining room. "I am the bringer of pancakes."

Nathan gasped. "Maria, you're a goddess."

Gabriel nodded. "She is. But don't tell her that — it'll go to her head."

"It already has," Maria replied dryly, pouring syrup.

They all ate together at the dining table — Tyler swinging his legs, Gabriel resting his foot against Nathan's under the table, and Nathan feeling… something he had never felt before.

Safe. Seen. Whole.

Halfway through breakfast, Tyler looked up. "So… are we all living together now?"

Gabriel paused mid-sip. Nathan swallowed a piece of pancake.

Nathan gently asked, "Do you want that?"

Tyler nodded instantly. "Yes. Because then I can show you guys my new school projects. And Daddy won't have to miss any more stuff. And you can help me build the biggest LEGO T. rex ever."

Nathan glanced at Gabriel. Gabriel looked like he might cry.

"Yes," Gabriel said softly. "We're living together."

Tyler grinned so wide it practically wrapped around his entire head.

Later that morning, as they gathered in the living room to talk about wedding ideas, Tyler suddenly yelled:

"OH NO!"

Nathan and Gabriel jumped.

Tyler stared at the coffee table in horror. "I knocked over my LEGO tower!"

It had indeed fallen — pieces scattered everywhere.

Gabriel smiled gently. "Watch this."

He flicked his fingers.

The silver amulet at his chest shimmered — and the LEGO bricks lifted themselves off the floor, gently swirling back into place. The tower rebuilt itself neatly on the table.

Tyler gasped so loudly he nearly fell over.

"DADDY CAN USE THE FORCE?!"

Gabriel grinned modestly. "Something like that."

Tyler turned to Nathan. "Can you do magic too?!"

Nathan looked at the amulet around his neck. "Well… a little."

He whispered the activation phrase only he could hear.

Time paused.

The dust in the air froze mid-float. The curtains froze mid-sway. Tyler froze mid-blink.

But Gabriel — bonded to the same energy — kept moving, watching Nathan with a soft smile.

Nathan gently picked Tyler up, carried him to the top of the stairs, sat him down with the plush raptor back in his arms, and kissed his forehead. Nathan then walked slowly back down to the living room area, sat for a few seconds and snapped his fingers, releasing the hold.

Time resumed.

Tyler blinked. Looked at his arms. Saw the raptor.

"WOAH. HOW DID—"

Nathan winked. "A magician never reveals his secrets."

Tyler ran down the stairs and threw himself into Nathan's arms. "YOU'RE THE COOLEST PAPA EVER."

Nathan laughed, hugging him close. Warmth flooded him like sunlight.

Gabriel whispered into Nathan's ear, "Careful. He's going to ask you to freeze time every time he loses a sock."

Nathan whispered back, "I'll do it."

Gabriel kissed his cheek. "I know."

As Tyler built the LEGO T. rex on the rug, Gabriel and Nathan sat on the couch with a notebook and a pair of matching smiles.

"So," Gabriel said, "beach wedding?"

"Hmm." Nathan tapped the pen. "Forest wedding?"

"Mountain wedding?"

"Castle wedding?"

They both laughed.

Tyler piped up from the floor, "Can we have DINOSAURS at the wedding?!"

Nathan considered. "Honestly… maybe."

Gabriel rubbed his face. "Please don't give him ideas."

"TOO LATE!" Tyler shouted.

Nathan leaned into Gabriel. "You know… this is better than anything I imagined."

Gabriel wrapped an arm around him and pulled him close. "This is only the beginning."

Gabriel stepped out to take Claire's call, leaving Nathan and Tyler on the living room rug, building dinosaurs side-by-side.

Tyler was quieter now. Not sad. Just… thinking.

Nathan could almost feel the gears turning as he looked at Tyler with a sideways glance.

Finally, Tyler put down a LEGO piece, grabbed his plush raptor, and crawled into Nathan's lap — not with excitement this time, but with a strange, hesitant seriousness.

Nathan's heart tightened.

"Hey, buddy," he murmured. "What's going on?"

Tyler looked down at the raptor in his hands, twisting its tail slowly. When he finally looked up, his eyes were deeper than any ten-year-old's should ever be.

While his right hand grasped my shirt, "Papa Nathan… if you and Daddy ever fight… and you get mad at each other… will you leave us?"

Nathan felt the question like a punch to the ribs.

His mouth opened before his mind caught up. "Tyler—no. No, sweetheart, I—I won't leave because of a fight."

Tyler continued staring at him, waiting.

"But," Nathan added slowly, "people… people don't always agree. It happens. But I stay. I talk things out. I work things through. I don't run."

Tyler blinked, processing.

Nathan felt a cold wave crawl up the back of his neck.

He wasn't sure he answered enough.

Tyler's fingers tightened on Nathan's shirt.

"But if you get *really* mad… or if Daddy gets mad… or if you get sad… or if… if I do something wrong…"

His voice cracked. "Will you go away then? Will you stop wanting me?"

Nathan felt something break in him.

He raised Tyler gently up some, so they were eye to eye.

"No," he said softly. "No, Tyler. Not for anger. Not for sadness. Not for mistakes. Not for anything you do or don't do."

Tyler swallowed. "People say that. But people still go."

Nathan felt his throat close.

He wanted to give the perfect words.

The unshakeable, flawless promise.

But he knew, deep inside, that humans weren't perfect — that he wasn't perfect — that life wasn't perfect.

So he gave the truest thing he had.

"I can't promise I'll never mess up," Nathan whispered. "Or that I'll never make mistakes.

But I *can* promise this: even if something goes wrong, even if Daddy and I get upset, even if I get scared… I don't give up on people I love."

Tyler's eyes softened — but he didn't look fully convinced.

Nathan felt that too.

He pulled Tyler into a tight hug.

"And you," Nathan whispered into his ear, "are someone I love. I'm staying. Even when it's hard. Even when it's messy. I'm not going anywhere. But… I know that maybe… it'll take time for you to believe that."

Tyler whispered against Nathan's chest: "…okay."

He didn't say "I believe you." He didn't say "I trust you."

He said, "Okay."

A brave little boy accepting the answer he got — even if part of him still wondered.

Nathan held him tighter, wishing he could fix every fear in one sentence.

He couldn't.

But he could stay.

Gabriel stood silently in the doorway, unseen, listening to the entire conversation.

His eyes were damp, his hand covering his mouth, his heart laid open.

Nathan didn't see him.

Tyler didn't see him.

But Gabriel saw and heard everything he needed to:

Nathan wasn't perfect. Nathan didn't give perfect answers.

Nathan gave honest ones.

And he stayed.

Nathan didn't hear Gabriel approach.

He was still sitting cross-legged on the rug, Tyler curled against his chest, small arms wound around his shirt as if they were the only thing keeping him anchored to the moment.

Tyler's breaths had softened into sleep — small, uneven at first, then settling into the steady rhythm of a child who'd finally run out of worry.

Nathan brushed Tyler's hair back, kissed his temple, and whispered something soft and warm.

That's when Gabriel finally stepped forward.

Nathan looked up suddenly, startled. "Oh—hey. I didn't see you."

Gabriel didn't answer right away.

He sat beside Nathan on the rug, slowly, like he wasn't sure his knees would cooperate.

Nathan blinked, noticing Gabriel's expression — the softness around the eyes, but also something heavier underneath.

Worry. Ache. Reverence.

"Gabriel?" Nathan whispered. "What is it?"

Gabriel looked at him the way a person looks at a sunrise after too many storms.

"I heard everything," he said softly.

Nathan stiffened. "Oh. I—did I say something wrong? Did I answer wrong? Gabriel, I tried, but I don't know if I—"

Gabriel gently placed a hand on his cheek.

"You didn't do anything wrong."

Nathan swallowed hard.

Gabriel looked down at his sleeping son for a moment, brushing Tyler's curls with the back of his fingers.

Then he spoke — quiet, fragile, honest.

"What Tyler asked you… that wasn't just a kid's question. That was a wound talking." He inhaled shakily. "And hearing it hurt more than anything has hurt me in a long time."

Nathan's heart tightened. "Because he asked if I'd leave…?"

Gabriel nodded.

"And because it means he's been afraid of that long before you came along."

Nathan's chest tightened painfully.

"Gabriel... I didn't realize—"

"You couldn't have known," Gabriel said. "But I should have. I'm his father. I should have seen that fear in him. I should have—"

"Stop." Nathan pressed a hand gently to Gabriel's chest. "You're a good dad. Kids get scared of things even when they're loved. Even when they're safe."

Gabriel lowered his head, voice thin.

"But I wasn't always here. Missions, nights away, months when contact was limited... he learned to prepare for people not coming home."

Nathan swallowed the ache rising in his throat.

"And hearing him ask you those questions," Gabriel continued, "made me realize how much he's been carrying. Alone."

Nathan felt his eyes sting.

"And then," Gabriel said, looking at him fully now, "I heard you answer."

Nathan opened his mouth — unsure.

Gabriel squeezed his hand.

"You didn't try to give a perfect promise. You didn't lie to make him feel better. You didn't say 'I'll never leave no matter what' like some storybook hero."

Gabriel's voice cracked softly.

"You told him the truth. The real truth. That you'll make mistakes. That humans fight. That you're not perfect. And that you stay anyway. That you fight for the people you love instead of abandoning them."

A tear slipped down Gabriel's cheek.

"You gave him something better than perfection, Nathan. You gave him honesty. You gave him something he can trust."

Nathan's own tears fell, gentle but unstoppable.

"I didn't know if it was enough," he whispered.

Gabriel leaned in — forehead resting against Nathan's.

"It was more than enough."

Nathan exhaled shakily. "And you? Why did it make you sad?"

Gabriel closed his eyes.

"Because for the first time," he whispered, "I realized I'm not doing this alone anymore. I'm not the only one protecting him. Loving him. Carrying his fears. You're here. You're staying. And hearing you love him — really love him — touches places in me I didn't know were still open."

Nathan's breath hitched.

The moment settled around them — deep, warm, tender.

Tyler slept between them, safe in the arms of a family he didn't have to question anymore.

Nathan wiped Gabriel's cheek gently. "Come here," he whispered.

Gabriel leaned into him, chest pressing against Nathan's shoulder as Nathan held him quietly.

They sat like that — a father, his partner, and the child they both loved — wrapped in a stillness that felt like healing.

Because tonight, a family didn't just form.

A family *came home.*

(18) CASTLES AND SHADOWS

The morning sunlight spilled across Gabriel's kitchen table as the three of them settled in with tea, juice, and a notebook labeled "Wedding Ideas (the Official Edition)."

Nathan flipped open the first page. "Okay, gentlemen. Venue."

Gabriel smirked. "Gentlemen? You're adorable."

Tyler puffed his chest. "Yes, we are *gentlemen.* Continue, Papa Nathan."

Nathan grinned. "All right. When I was Tyler's age—"

"Ten?" Tyler asked.

"Yes, ten," Nathan said, leaning back dreamily, "I used to imagine that I would grow up, dress like a Disney prince — cape, boots, embroidered jacket, the whole dramatic ensemble — and I'd marry another prince in a castle somewhere."

Gabriel paused mid-sip. "You wanted to marry a prince?"

Nathan nodded. "I did. Not just any prince, though. A brave one. One who looked at me like I was worth crossing a kingdom for."

Gabriel reached under the table and squeezed his hand.

Tyler's eyes widened. "So you wanted, like... a *real castle* wedding?"

Nathan chuckled. "In my mind? Absolutely. I imagined the big stone towers, stained glass, trumpets playing, and everyone wearing enchanted outfits."

Tyler practically vibrated. "Can we go see the Disney castle today?! Like right now?! There's no school today!"

Gabriel raised an eyebrow. "Well... we *could.*"

Nathan blinked. "We really could. I mean... why not? We can do a little 'venue scouting.'"

Tyler gasped. "And shop for prince costumes!"

Nathan laughed. "We might need them custom-made, but we can get ideas."

Gabriel stood and stretched. "Well then. Road trip."

Tyler scrambled toward the door. "I'll get my shoes!"

Nathan watched him run down the hall, his heart feeling far too full.

Gabriel wrapped an arm around Nathan's waist. "You wanted a castle wedding when you were ten?"

Nathan nodded. "Yes."

Gabriel kissed the side of his head. "Let's go see your childhood dream."

The Disney theme park bustled with families, balloons, and the aroma of popcorn and sweet pastries. But as they approached the towering spires of the castle, something inside Nathan stilled.

It really did look like the castle from his childhood dream — blue rooftops, white stone, banners fluttering in the breeze. It was imaginative, whimsical, and enchanting.

Tyler grabbed both of their hands. "It's perfect!"

Nathan laughed, exhilarated. "It really is."

They walked through the grand archway, the echoing acoustics making the space feel otherworldly. Gift shops glittered with crowns, capes, and costume displays. Tyler darted around, trying on plastic helmets and waving foam swords.

Nathan turned slowly in the center of the hall, taking everything in. "When I was little, I imagined walking down an aisle right here," he said. "Music playing, lights glowing, the whole world watching magic happen."

Gabriel placed a hand at the small of his back. "We can make that happen."

Nathan swallowed hard, emotional. "You mean it?"

Gabriel smiled softly. "I'll marry you anywhere. But if this is your childhood dream? Then yes. Especially here."

Nathan leaned his head briefly on Gabriel's shoulder.

Tyler rushed back, dragging a comically oversized prince cape behind him. "WE NEED THESE FOR THE WEDDING!"

Nathan laughed. "Maybe something a little more tailored, buddy."

Tyler frowned thoughtfully. "Custom-made?"

"Exactly."

Everything was warm and bright and full of laughter—until Tyler stopped in his tracks.

A tall figure in flowing black-and-red robes drifted into view near the throne display. His twisted staff glinted. His painted eyebrows arched dramatically.

Jafar, the evil wizard from the timeless tale of Disney's Aladdin.

Or rather, a very enthusiastic park actor *playing* Jafar.

He slithered toward families, twirling his staff, speaking in a booming theatrical voice, clearly loving every second of his villain role.

When he spotted Tyler staring wide-eyed, he smirked under the makeup.

"Well, well, well," Jafar purred, approaching with exaggerated menace, "I smell fear in the air. Who do we have here? A little street rat trying to invade my palace?"

Tyler shrank back instinctively.

Nathan's entire body tensed.

Gabriel straightened, jaw tightening.

Jafar leaned closer, tapping Tyler's shoulder with the tip of his staff. "Run along now, boy, before I turn you into—"

Nathan stepped between them so fast the actor blinked.

"That's close enough," Nathan said, voice low.

Jafar laughed, thinking it was all part of the immersive fun. "Ohhh, protective papa! How delightful. Do you fear the great—"

Gabriel moved beside Nathan, not smiling. "Back up," he said calmly.

The actor faltered for the first time. "Sir, it's— it's just entertainment."

"Not for him," Nathan replied, eyes sharp.

Tyler peeked from behind Nathan's waist, small hands gripping his sleeve.

Jafar softened slightly, realizing the kid was genuinely afraid— but he tried to stay in character.

"Oh, come now," he said, reaching out dramatically as if to scare him again.

Gabriel didn't let him finish.

The silver amulet at his chest glimmered.

FWUP.

Jafar lifted off the ground.

His feet kicked in the air, robe dangling ridiculously as he hovered several feet up.

"What—WHAT—WHAT IS HAPPENING?!" he shrieked, dropping his staff.

Gabriel crossed his arms. "You don't scare our kid."

Jafar wobbled helplessly in mid-air. "Sir! I—this—this is not in my contract!"

Nathan sighed, cracked his knuckles, and whispered the activation phrase.

Time stopped.

Curtains froze mid-flutter. Families paused mid-step. A popcorn kernel hung suspended in midair.

Gabriel and Jafar were the only other beings still in motion—Gabriel because of his bond to the anomaly, Jafar because Gabriel was physically holding him in a gravity-detached state.

Nathan walked casually toward the castle's moat, motioning Gabriel over.

"Bring him," Nathan said, smirking.

Gabriel floated the flailing actor behind him like a large, screaming balloon.

They reached the edge of the moat.

Nathan crouched, examining the water. "Refreshing."

"Oh no," Jafar whimpered. "No, no, please—don't do anything rash! I have sensitive sinuses—"

Nathan placed a gentle finger on the actor's forehead. "This," Nathan said sweetly, "is a lesson."

"Wh—WHAT LESSON?!" the actor begged.

Nathan smiled brightly. "Don't. Mess. With. Our. Kid."

He snapped his fingers.

Time resumed.

Families screamed in shock as a grown man in a full Jafar costume suddenly appeared dangling upside down over the moat.

Gabriel released him.

SPLASH!

A wave erupted.

The actor surfaced sputtering, eyeliner streaking, turban floating away.

A nearby cast member shouted, "JAFAR WHAT THE—"

"HELP!" the actor wailed. "THESE TWO MEN HAVE—THEY—THEY—!"

But a lifeguard was already rushing over, lowering a pole.

Gabriel tugged Nathan back toward Tyler while the soaked villain was helped out of the water.

Nathan knelt to Tyler's level.

"You okay, kiddo?" he asked, brushing a curl off Tyler's forehead.

Tyler nodded slowly. "Yeah. Because you're both here."

Nathan hugged him. "Always."

Gabriel placed a hand on Tyler's back. "And no one, not even Disney villains," he said, "gets to scare you."

Tyler beamed. "You guys are the BEST."

Maria would've had a heart attack.

Claire would definitely need a drink.

But Nathan and Gabriel?

They walked back into the sunshine of the castle courtyard holding Tyler's hands, leaving a dripping, traumatized Jafar behind them.

Nathan whispered to Gabriel as they walked:

"Think we went too far?"

Gabriel shrugged. "He'll dry."

Tyler added proudly, "And Papa Nathan and Daddy are superheroes."

Nathan smiled, squeezing both their hands.

"Yeah," he whispered, "we kind of are."

(19) ROYAL FITTINGS & FAMILY OF CHOICE

Nathan wasn't sure who shouted first — Tyler, or Hailey.

Because the moment Gabriel, Nathan, and Tyler stepped out of the costume shop into the sunlight of the park's "Fantasy Village," a familiar voice shrieked:

"NATHAAAAN!"

Before Nathan could even blink, a blur of bright hair and boundless energy launched itself at him like a missile.

"HAILEY?!" Nathan laughed, stumbling a step back as she wrapped him in the tightest hug known to mankind. "How are you even here?!"

She pulled away dramatically. "Sweetheart, you're planning a CASTLE WEDDING. Did you think I wouldn't appear like a fairy godmother on steroids?"

Gabriel snorted. Tyler giggled. Nathan pretended to wipe sweat off his forehead.

Hailey crouched dramatically in front of Tyler. "And YOU must be the famous Tyler I've heard about. Tell me everything. Favorite colors. Favorite dinosaurs. Favorite snacks. Go."

Tyler blinked, then instinctively warmed to her spark.

"Uh—blue, T. rex, and strawberry yogurt."

Hailey gasped. "We're soulmates. Come with me, tiny prince."

She held out her hand. Tyler took it instantly.

Nathan blinked. "She's… she's adopted him in three seconds."

Gabriel smiled. "That's Hailey."

Hailey dragged the entire family back inside the costume & wardrobe hall — a massive backstage-style building filled with mirrors, mannequins, fabrics, capes, embroidery samples, and racks upon racks of princely attire.

"This," Hailey announced, sweeping her arms theatrically, "is where magic meets tailoring. And THIS—" She pointed to Nathan. "—is where your dream wedding LOOK begins."

Nathan blushed. Gabriel smirked. Tyler grabbed a scepter.

A tailor hurried over, bowing so low he nearly curled into a circle.

"Chief Enchantment Realm Director & President Nathan," he said breathlessly, "you honor us. Please — anything you desire."

Nathan leaned toward Gabriel. "That title feels… cushy."

Gabriel whispered, "You deserve it."

Hailey clapped her hands. "Okay, Director & President Nathan — let's get you looking like the king you are."

Nathan felt his stomach flip. "Right. Measurements. Great."

What followed could only be described as: Chaos. Glorious, sparkly, tailor-scattered chaos.

Nathan stood on a raised platform while Hailey circled him like a hawk wearing glitter eyeliner.

"We need a deeper navy on the cape. He looks good in the white suit. Add a golden vest and gold decoration on the coat too. Golden embroidery looks nice. Maybe a celestial motif. Something that says 'I freeze time and still look good doing it.'"

Nathan choked on a laugh. "I do not look good freezing time."

Gabriel leaned against the wall, arms crossed, eyes filled with warmth. "You do, actually."

Nathan's ears turned pink.

Tailors bustled around Gabriel next — measuring shoulders, inseam, wingspan (which confused him).

"Hovering requires flexibility," one tailor explained.

Gabriel sighed. "This is so unnecessary."

Hailey shouted, "You are marrying a PRINCE. You will look SUPERNATURAL." She made more notes in her notebook and then told the tailor, "Maybe more silver embellishment on his lapels and seams of his golden coat, and just keep his amber cape simple, not heavily laden with frills."

Tyler clung to Hailey's other side, pointing at different fabrics.

"And Papa Nathan needs sparkles here," he said, pointing to the collar.

Nathan groaned. "Tyler, buddy—"

"It's important," Tyler insisted seriously.

Hailey nodded firmly. "The kid's right. A subtle shimmer on both yours and Gabriel's collars."

Then came Tyler's turn.

He stepped onto the platform proudly.

Hundreds of fabrics swirled around him like a rainbow tornado.

"I want to be a little prince too," he declared confidently.

"You ARE one," Nathan said, lifting him gently. "Your suite will be a miniature of your dad's. You'll look just like him, minus the cape cuz you can't fly." And just like that, Tyler made a face at

Papa Nathan and a smirk like, 'You're gonna get it when I get free'.

Tailors giggled as they measured Tyler, who kept puffing his chest to look "more princely."

Hailey sketched at lightning speed — sweeping lines, bold shoulders, miniature capes, high collars.

Her designs were stunning.

"Nathan," she said, holding up a sketch, "this style will make you look kingly. Regal. Ethereal. This says, 'I bend time and marry the man of my dreams.'"

Nathan's throat tightened.

He looked at Gabriel, who looked at him like he was already wearing the whole outfit.

Word spread fast.

Staff began arriving with trays of refreshments — gold-rimmed glasses, velvet cupcakes, chilled mango tea.

Musicians appeared, tuning harps.

Squires in training offered to polish Gabriel's boots.

Someone presented Tyler with a gorgeous golden crown "for inspiration."

Nathan whispered, "I think they're overdoing it."

A coordinator bowed deeply. "Chief Enchantment Realm Director & President, we could *never* overdo your service."

Gabriel nearly choked laughing.

Nathan rubbed his forehead. "Okay, everyone — let's not put the kid on a throne yet."

Tyler, already sitting on a throne, shouted, "TOO LATE!"

There were awkward bits.

- Nathan squeaked when a tailor tightened the measuring tape.
- Gabriel nearly levitated a man on reflex when someone grabbed his thigh unexpectedly.
- Tyler stabbed himself lightly with a safety pin and then declared he was "bravely wounded."
- Hailey attempted to mark fabric with a pencil while a tailor was still measuring Gabriel's inseam, causing Gabriel to jump so high he nearly hovered.
- Nathan froze time once to stop a tray of pastries from falling, then pretended nothing happened.

But in the end?

Every outfit had been chosen. Measurements recorded. Designs finalized. Fabric ordered from realms no human tailor had ever accessed.

And Hailey stood proudly between them all, hands on her hips.

"This," she said triumphantly, "is going to be the wedding of the century."

Nathan smiled at her — at Tyler, who was twirling in a prototype cape, and at Gabriel, whose expression softened with quiet happiness.

"We're really doing this," Nathan whispered.

Gabriel slipped an arm around him.

"We are," he said softly. "And it's going to be unforgettable."

Tyler tugged Nathan's shirt sleeve.

"Papa Nathan?"

"Yes, little prince?"

Tyler grinned. "Can I practice walking down the aisle with my cape?"

Nathan laughed.

"You can practice as much as you want."

And as Tyler scampered away, cape swishing, Hailey scribbling more designs, Gabriel watching with a proud smile…

Nathan felt it again.

That warm, glowing truth:

He had a family. He had a future. And he had a whole enchanted realm at his fingertips — but none of it mattered more than the two people standing beside him.

(20) THE REHEARSAL OF HEARTS

The rehearsal dinner was held in the grand hall Nathan had chosen — a sweeping space beneath chandeliers that shimmered like suspended constellations. Long banquet tables curved around the room in gentle arcs, draped in velvet and gold. Musicians warmed up at the far end, testing harps and soft percussion.

Nathan walked in with Gabriel and Tyler at his side, Hailey flouncing in behind them like a choreographed whirlwind.

"Places, everyone!" she shouted, waving her clipboard. "But also ignore me. I'm just here to cause chaos."

Nathan's personal assistant, Henrik, skidded past Hailey with a mountain of notes under his arm, hair sticking up like he had run face-first through a wind tunnel.

"Everyone stay calm!" Henrik barked. "We have timelines! We have décor placements! We have EMERGENCIES!"

Hailey flounced behind him. "Henrik, sweetie, you're vibrating."

"I have REASONS," Henrik snapped, then immediately softened. "But also I'm having the BEST day."

Hailey mock-bowed. "Your kingdom, Your Highness. Lead us."

Henrik froze, straightened his spine, and shouted, "I AM IN CHARGE!"

Then a server dropped a tray and Henrik shrieked, running off like a frantic rooster.

Hailey turned to Nathan. "I adore him."

Nathan sighed. "He's… enthusiastic."

Gabriel leaned in. "That's one word for it."

Tailors attempted to measure Gabriel's arm while Henrik tried directing them like an air traffic controller.

"No! No! His left arm is the dramatic arm! More structure there!"

"Henrik," Hailey said, patting his head, "sweetheart, breathe."

"I *AM* breathing!" he insisted, immediately tripping over fabric and popping back up like a spring.

Nathan laughed.

"He loves this. Every chaotic second."

"And I love mocking him," Hailey added. "It's how I show affection."

Claire stepped through the doors, wearing a simple but elegant dress — the kind that said she wanted to look nice, but not outshine the moment.

"Hey," Gabriel said, pulling her into a hug.

"You made it."

"Of course I did," Claire smiled. "You're my family."

Tyler rushed in, clinging to her waist. "Mom! Mom! You get to see the outfits!"

Claire laughed. "I'm excited, sweetheart."

Nathan stepped forward warmly. "We have something for you first."

Two attendants — dressed in royal blue — approached with a long velvet box.

"Nathan," Claire breathed, "what is this?"

"Open it."

She did.

Inside, cushioned in gold satin, was the most breathtaking regalia she had ever seen:

A delicate silver tiara lined with small gemstones that glimmered like captured starlight. A sleek scepter tipped with a crystal sphere. A sequined gown in midnight black with gold threads woven through the hem. A light shoulder cape that flowed like a wisp of moonlight.

Claire's hands flew to her mouth.

"I—I can't wear this," she whispered, overwhelmed. "It's too much. It's—this is—it's for someone important."

Nathan shook his head gently.

"It's for you," he said softly. "For everything you've given. Everything you've done. Everything you've carried alone. You deserve to feel like royalty tonight."

Claire's breath hitched — and tears spilled down her cheeks without warning.

"Oh sweetheart," Nathan murmured, pulling her into a warm embrace, easing her into Gabriel's arms as well.

Tyler wrapped himself around her waist again. "Mommy… don't cry. You're a queen."

Claire laughed through her tears. "Oh, baby… thank you."

Nathan placed a gentle hand against her cheek.

"You raised an extraordinary young man. You sacrificed so much. And the more I know Tyler, the more I see how much love you poured into him. You're just as much a part of this family as any of us. We honor that tonight."

Claire folded into him with a quiet sob — relief, gratitude, and acceptance washing through her like a tide.

She wasn't losing a son. She was gaining a family.

Once Claire donned her regal ensemble — and looked *every bit* the queen Tyler insisted she was — the fitting madness began.

Tailors swarmed the room, adjusting hems, tracing chalk lines, and trying desperately to get people to stand still.

Hailey kept sabotaging Henrik.

While he tried to measure Gabriel's sleeve, she whispered, "Too short."

So he lengthened it.

"Actually too long."

He shortened it.

"Henrik, darling," Hailey said, leaning around Gabriel, "have you considered taking over my job?"

Henrik puffed up. "Really?"

"No," she said sweetly.

Gabriel nearly choked laughing.

Tyler practiced his cape swish in the corner, knocking over exactly three goblets and one chair.

Claire gasped. "My little prince… maybe *less* swish."

Tyler swished harder.

Halfway through dinner, the musicians started a soft melody.
Nathan froze.

It was a song his mother used to hum — a tune woven into his childhood, etched into every hopeful corner of his heart.

Something inside him unlocked.

He stepped onto the open floor. Gabriel watched him from the table, curiosity turning to awe.

Nathan closed his eyes. And he began to dance.

Not a performance. Not a routine. A release.

A celebration.

His arms stretched wide, sweeping the air like he was gathering the entire room into a single embrace. He spun, leapt, twisted — graceful and powerful all at once.

Light shimmered around him.

Hailey stopped in mid-bite. Claire covered her heart. Tyler gasped. "HE CAN FLY TOO??"

Gabriel's eyes widened.

And with every leap, Nathan rose slightly higher than gravity should've allowed. Barely an inch. Then two.

Then, during a sweeping turn— Nathan's foot didn't return to the floor for seven or more rotations.

He held it in the air for just an extended breath.

Gabriel's throat closed.

He wasn't imagining it.

Nathan was *lifting*.

Effortlessly. Unconsciously. Beautifully.

As if the dance and the amulet were working in unison, honoring the moment.

Nathan's final spin landed softly — breathless, glowing, tears in his eyes.

The room erupted in applause.

Gabriel stood, unable to stop himself, and wrapped Nathan in his arms. "I've never seen anything so beautiful," he whispered. "You danced with your whole soul."

Nathan swallowed hard. "I felt… free."

Tyler ran up, grabbing Nathan's hand excitedly.

"Papa Nathan! Can you teach me? Can you teach me flips? And leaping? And floating?!"

Nathan laughed. "I can teach you gymnastics. And stretching. And maybe… whatever this new thing is."

Tyler beamed. "YES!"

As the room drifted into dessert and laughter, Nathan stepped out onto the balcony for air.

The night was warm. Candles flickered. Music carried softly through the doors.

Nathan looked up at the stars.

"Marcus," he whispered, voice barely a breath. "You should've been here."

A quiet sadness touched his smile.

"You would've teased me for crying, told me my cape was too long, and pretended you didn't like Gabriel until he did something to impress you."

He exhaled, eyes soft.

"I miss you. But I know you'd be proud. I'm building something beautiful now. Something real."

A tear traced down his cheek.

Gabriel stepped behind him, sliding his arms around his waist.

"Are you okay?" he asked gently.

Nathan nodded. "I'm good. Just remembering someone who helped me become who I am."

Gabriel kissed his cheek. "They're part of this too. Every piece of your story brought you here."

Nathan leaned back into him.

"Yeah," he whispered. "Yeah, it did."

And together they watched the night sky, surrounded by family, by laughter, by magic, and by the promise of the life they were about to begin.

(21) THE ROYAL UNION OF TWO PRINCES

The sun rose over the Enchanted Realm with a softness that felt almost reverent — as if the sky itself understood what the day meant. Gold light spilled across the castle spires, warming the stained-glass windows and casting shimmering reflections into the courtyard below.

Inside the grand hall, everything glowed.

Velvet drapes the color of twilight, framing the aisle. Silver lanterns floated midair, gently circling above the guests. Musicians tuned harps and crystal chimes that sang with magic. The air thrummed with expectation, with blessings, with love.

Tyler stood at the front in his custom-made little prince suit, cape and all, proudly clutching the wedding bands. His chin lifted with princely seriousness — even though he'd clearly eaten three cupcakes already.

Hailey bustled about with a clipboard, hair sparkling with stardust confetti.

Claire, regal in her sequined gown and shoulder cape, wore the tiara Nathan had given her. She glowed like a queen from a storybook — one who had earned every jewel through strength and grace.

Henrik was in full meltdown mode.

"Places! Everyone! Sparkles to the left, candles to the right — WHO MOVED THE SCEPTER?!"

Hailey whispered loudly, "Henrik, I moved it."

"You WHAT—?!"

"To see if I could break you."

Henrik inhaled deeply. "I love my job. I love my job. I LOVE MY JOB." He shrieked.

Gabriel stood behind a carved pillar, adjusting his ceremonial jacket — silver embroidery, celestial patterns, and a high collar that made him look both royal and dangerous in all the right ways. His amulet rested against his chest, glowing faintly.

He looked powerful.

He looked breathtaking.

He looked like a prince.

But the moment he heard soft footsteps behind him, his breath caught.

Nathan stepped into the light.

Nathan's wedding attire shimmered like living starlight.

Deep navy fabric woven with silver constellations. A cape that flowed behind him like dusk falling into the night. A high collar lined in subtle gemstones. Silver embroidery like frozen waves running down the sleeves.

He looked ethereal. Timeless. As if the amulet around his neck was part of him — not something he wore, but something that responded to him.

Gabriel forgot how to breathe.

Nathan stopped beside him, cheeks pink.

"Hey," he whispered.

Gabriel swallowed. "You look… radiant."

Nathan laughed quietly, nerves humming in his voice. "You clean up pretty well yourself."

They didn't kiss. Not yet.

But they touched foreheads gently, sharing a breath.

"This is really happening," Nathan murmured.

"It's happening," Gabriel whispered back. "With you. Always with you."

Music swelled — a soft, magical melody carried by harps and shimmering chimes.

Guests rose.

Tyler gasped. "It's time!"

The grand doors opened.

Nathan and Gabriel stepped forward together — not separately, not meeting at the altar, but walking side by side.

A symbolic choice.

Two princes. Two equals. Two hearts choosing each other freely.

The castle itself seemed to glow brighter. Light followed them down the aisle. Even the air felt warmer, gilded with magic.

Claire dabbed her eyes. Hailey fanned her face dramatically. Henrik fainted briefly, then popped back up like a jack-in-the-box.

At the altar, they turned to face one another — hands brushing, fingertips trembling slightly.

The officiant, dressed in shimmering robes, lifted his staff.

"Today," he said, voice deep and rhythmic, "we witness a union that transcends kingdom and realm. A love forged in courage, shaped by sacrifice, strengthened by truth."

He looked at Gabriel.

"And you, Gabriel — do you vow to walk beside Nathan not as a guardian, but as a partner? To protect without possession, to love without fear, to share your heart and your home and your future?"

Gabriel stepped closer, eyes shining.

"I do," he whispered. "I have since the moment he saved me from myself."

The officiant turned to Nathan.

"And you, Nathan — do you vow to walk beside Gabriel not as a keeper, but as a companion? To cherish without condition, to honor without hesitation, to lift him when he falters and love him when he doubts?"

Nathan's breath trembled.

"I do," he said softly. "And I promise… I'll never run. Not from him. Not from us."

Tyler stepped forward, holding the rings with all the solemnity of a royal guard.

"Here," he whispered proudly.

Gabriel slid the band onto Nathan's finger — silver, sapphire-lined.

Nathan slid Gabriel's ring on — molten silver, etched with Gabriel's crest.

Their amulets glowed in unison.

The officiant raised his staff.

"Then by the power of the Enchanted Realm, the blessing of the anomalies who witnessed your bond, and the hearts of everyone who loves you — I declare your union sealed."

He smiled.

"You may kiss your prince."

Gabriel didn't hesitate.

He pulled Nathan close, cupped his cheek, and kissed him — deep, tender, and full of everything they'd been through.

The crowd erupted.

Magic burst like fireworks overhead — shimmering threads of light spiraling across the ceiling.

And then—

Nathan lifted slightly off the ground. Just an inch.

Gabriel lifted with him.

Their rings glowed. Their amulets pulsed together, glimmering, glowing, and even exchanging, morphing, and joining in the moment beyond that place. The embodied power grew, strengthened, and added power unto their wearers. Their bodies hovered in a gentle, weightless embrace. And for a moment or two, they vanished, only to reappear lowering.

When they lowered, Tyler screamed, "BEST. WEDDING. EVER!"

Hailey sobbed dramatically. Claire pressed a hand to her heart. Henrik fainted again.

Nathan leaned into Gabriel and whispered, "We're really married."

Gabriel kissed him softly. "We're really married."

And as applause thundered through the hall, Nathan knew:

Every broken moment in his life had led him here. To this man. To this family. To this love…eternally. Nathan turned toward their guests, breath still unsteady from the kiss, from the magic, from the pure enormity of becoming someone's forever.

"And now," Nathan began, voice shining as brightly as the amulet at his chest, "we have one more ring to bestow. A promise ring… for Gabriel's son, Tyler."

The room fell instantly quiet — a reverent hush.

Gabriel's head snapped toward Nathan, eyes widening, heart already in his throat.

Nathan continued, a softness threading through every word. "This ring is our promise to you, Tyler. A promise that you will always be loved, always supported, always protected. That your growing-up years will be surrounded by stability and joy. This ring means you are not just part of this wedding…"

Nathan's voice wavered, warm and full. "…you are part of this marriage. Part of our family. Forever."

Tyler blinked up at him — small, brave, and suddenly overwhelmed by emotion he didn't fully understand but absolutely felt.

Gabriel's breath caught; tears pricked his eyes. He reached for Nathan's hand without thinking, gripping it like a lifeline.

Nathan smiled through the ache blooming in his chest. "A royal wedding deserves royal promises. And this is ours to you."

For a heartbeat, Tyler just stared — wide-eyed, unmoving, as if trying to understand whether this moment was truly meant for him.

Then his little face crumpled.

Not in fear. Not in confusion. But in that stunned, breathless sort of joy that children rarely have words for.

He ran forward — arms out, eyes shining.

"Papa Nathan… really?" his voice cracked.

Nathan knelt instantly, meeting him at eye level. "Really," he whispered. "This is your ring. Your promise. Our promise."

Gabriel joined them on the floor, one arm slipping around Tyler's shoulders, the other around Nathan's back — drawing all three into a single circle of warmth.

Nathan lifted the small velvet box and opened it. Inside lay a simple but elegant band of brushed silver, faintly etched with a pattern resembling tiny feathers — a quiet echo of the family symbol forming between them all.

Tyler gasped softly. "It's… mine?"

"It's yours," Gabriel said gently. "A promise we make together."

Nathan took Tyler's small hand and slid the ring onto his finger. It fit perfectly — not snug, not loose — as if it had known where it belonged all along.

The moment the ring settled into place, both Nathan's and Gabriel's amulets pulsed at once.

A soft, radiant glow rippled outward — not bright enough to blind, but warm enough to stir every heart in the room. The two amulets glimmered in perfect synchrony, threads of light extending between them like golden filaments…

…and then one last filament branched outward, arcing gently toward Tyler's small chest, touching lightly, lovingly, without harm.

Tyler inhaled sharply, a tiny spark of blue-white light shimmering at his sternum for just a second — not an amulet, not a gift he had to carry, but a *recognition*. A blessing. A bond.

A chosen child welcomed by chosen parents.

Gabriel pressed a trembling kiss into Tyler's hair. Nathan rested his forehead against both of them.

The glow faded slowly, leaving the hall stunned, hushed, reverent — as though they'd all witnessed something sacred.

Tyler sniffed, wiping his face with the back of his hand. "So… does this mean I'm really your kid?"

Nathan cupped his cheeks. "It means," he said gently, "you're ours. Today, tomorrow, and every day after."

Gabriel nodded, voice thick. "No exceptions. No conditions. You're an important part of our family."

Tyler launched into them again, hugging them so fiercely that even the guests laughed through their tears.

And above them, the faintest echo lingered in the air — not from the amulets, but from the love binding them all:

A royal wedding befitting two princes who truly, deeply loved — and the little prince who completed them.

(22) THE GLOWING RECEPTION

The moment Gabriel and Nathan touched down from their mid-air embrace — rings bright, amulets fused into a single luminous pattern against their chests — the entire hall erupted into applause so thunderous it nearly shook dust from the rafters.

Light still clung to them.

Not sunlight. Not candlelight. Something alive.

Something new.

Nathan pressed a hand to his chest. The merged amulet felt warm — not hot, not heavy, just *present*. Like it was breathing with him.

Gabriel's fingers brushed his. "I feel it too."

The officiant bowed his head reverently. "The anomalies have gifted you more than a union," he murmured. "They've given you a legacy."

Tyler beamed. "My dads have MAGIC 2.0!"

After the pronouncement of the ring to Tyler, the guests filtered into the reception hall — a space transformed into a celestial ballroom:

floating lanterns drifting like stars

tables draped in violet and silver

a floral archway glowing softly with enchantment

crystal glasses chiming like they were singing

Nathan and Gabriel entered hand in hand, and the room seemed to brighten as they stepped inside.

Tyler walked in with a bounce, ogling at his first real ring.

Claire dabbed her eyes again. Hailey hoisted her champagne glass dramatically. Henrik attempted a toast on a chair, fell off, and pretended it was intentional.

All as expected.

As Nathan walked, he felt something odd:

The air bent around him gently. Not in a way anyone else would notice — but he felt it.

Textures clearer. Movements smoother. The world is responding to his emotions.

Gabriel felt different, too.

He reached for a glass at the end of the bar.

Before he'd even lifted his hand fully…

…the glass floated gently into his palm.

He blinked.

Nathan raised an eyebrow. "No hand gesture?"

Gabriel whispered, "I think the amulet… upgraded me."

Nathan grinned. "Me too."

Tyler tugged Nathan's sleeve. "Papa Nathan, did you make the lanterns float? Or are they floaty because they're floaty?"

Nathan winked. "A little of both."

Music drifted into the air — soft piano, low harp, distant chimes. The kind of music that felt like a prayer and a celebration in one breath.

Nathan and Gabriel stepped onto the dance floor.

He expected to feel nervous. Self-conscious.

Instead…

Nathan felt weightless.

Literally.

Their steps flowed like water — When Gabriel guided him into a spin, Nathan's foot left the ground just a hair longer than human balance should allow.

Gabriel lifted him effortlessly — not with magic, but with love — and when their foreheads touched, the amulet glowed between them like a heartbeat turned to crystal.

Guests watched in awed silence.

The dance looked choreographed. Rehearsed. Stage-worthy.

But it was simply two people who had finally found the place in the world where they belonged.

Together.

The applause from their first dance was still fading when Tyler tugged eagerly on Nathan's sleeve.

"Papa Nathan," he whispered, eyes wide with hope, "can I dance with you too?"

Nathan felt his whole heart melt.

"Of course," he breathed. "Come here, my little prince."

Tyler clambered into Nathan's arms without hesitation and wrapped his legs around his midsection. Gabriel stepped back, smiling softly as the musicians shifted into a lighter, playful melody.

Nathan carried Tyler onto the dance floor.

"Ready?" Nathan asked.

Tyler nodded. "I trust you."

Nathan touched the merged amulet.

It warmed instantly.

And when Nathan lifted Tyler into the air, they floated.

Higher… and higher… gently rising like the two of them were being lifted by a dream.

Gasps rippled through the room. Claire covered her mouth. Hailey shouted, "OH MY GOD HE'S A SKY BOY-ANGEL!" Henrik fainted again.

Nathan held Tyler securely, laughing breathlessly as they twirled midair.

"You're flying!" Tyler yelled, joyful and radiant.

"No," Nathan corrected, brushing Tyler's cheek, "*we're* flying."

They spun slowly beneath the floating lanterns, drifting over the crowd like a starry waltz.

Tyler stretched his arms wide, cape fluttering behind him.

"I feel like a real prince!" he cried.

"You are," Nathan said softly. "And you always will be."

The amulet glowed brighter, shimmering threads of light trailing behind it like gentle comets.

After a slow, graceful arc through the air, Nathan brought them gliding back toward the ground — landing with a feather-soft touch.

Tyler hugged him fiercely.

"That was the best dance of my life."

Nathan kissed his forehead. "Mine too."

Gabriel stepped forward then — smiling, eyes bright.

"My turn."

Tyler blinked. "Really?"

Gabriel nodded, holding out his arms.

Tyler ran into them.

And in one smooth, effortless motion—

Gabriel lifted him…

…and floated upward just as gracefully as Nathan had.

But Gabriel's style was different — less ethereal, more powerful, sweeping Tyler in wide arcs that felt like windstorms.

Tyler shrieked with laughter.

"DADDY YOU'RE FAST!"

Gabriel grinned, spinning smoothly. "And strong."

Tyler hugged his neck as they spun through the air like two streaks of silver.

Claire wept happy tears. Nathan watched with a warmth that filled every corner of him.

Father and son drifted back to the ground in a final sweep, and Gabriel set Tyler down gently.

Tyler immediately grabbed both their hands.

"That was perfect," he said breathlessly. "You're the best dads in the whole world."

And for a moment, all three of them simply stood together —
glowing in the aftermath, wrapped in love, magic, and the kind
of joy that could lift anyone into the air.

After the dance, Hailey grabbed the mic.

"All right, peasants, shut up! The little prince has something to
say!"

Claire snorted. Henrik nearly fainted again.

Tyler climbed onto a small platform — his cape slightly crooked,
crown slipping sideways — and he held the microphone with
both hands.

"Um… hi," he said, voice quivering at first. "I'm Tyler."

The guests softened instantly.

"And… um… I want to say something about my dads."

Gabriel's breath caught. Nathan's hand pressed to his heart.

Tyler continued, voice growing steadier:

"My mom always told me that families come in all shapes and
sizes. But I didn't really believe her until now. Because… my
family didn't feel full before."

Nathan pressed his lips together hard. Gabriel blinked rapidly.

Tyler swallowed.

"I had love. And fun. And good days. But I always felt like
something was missing. And now I know what it was."

He looked at Nathan.

"You."

Nathan's breath broke.

Tyler kept going.

"You made Daddy smile in a different way. The way people smile when they're home. And you made me feel like… like I wasn't too much. Or too loud. Or too scared. You made me feel like I was strong."

Nathan's eyes flooded.

Gabriel was already crying.

"And today, when you danced… You looked like a hero. My hero. And Daddy's hero. And I'm really happy you married my dad. And I'm really happy you're my Papa. And…"

His voice cracked.

"And I'm really happy that we're a family now."

He wiped his cheeks quickly with his sleeve.

"I love you both."

Silence. Then — an explosion of applause, cheers, and sniffles.

Nathan scooped him off the stage, hugging him so tightly that Tyler squeaked.

Gabriel wrapped his arms around both of them.

And for a moment, the world was perfect.

The reception didn't last long.

Not because the guests were tired — But because Nathan and Gabriel weren't.

Not tonight.

Not after this day, this dance, this merging of power and destiny.

Claire kissed both their cheeks before leaving with Tyler. Hailey threatened to break into their room and film them. Henrik declared he "successfully managed chaos" and then fainted for real.

Finally — blissfully — the hall quieted.

Nathan and Gabriel slipped away through a side corridor lit by lanterns.

Their hands intertwined, fingers brushing the merged amulet between them.

Gabriel whispered, voice thick with emotion:

"We survived the world, Nathan."

Nathan whispered back:

"We *built* one."

The night was short.

But the hours they shared afterward — in tenderness, in passion, in whispered promises — were monumental.

The true beginning of their married life.

Their hearts. Their powers. Their souls.

Finally united.

(23) FIRST MORNING OF FOREVER

Nathan woke first.

For a long minute, he simply lay there — staring at the ceiling, letting the soft morning light drift across the sheets, feeling the warmth of the man sleeping beside him. Gabriel's arm was draped across his waist, his breath slow and even, his presence grounding and familiar in a new, indescribably powerful way.

Husband.

The word echoed in Nathan's mind like a prayer and a celebration all at once.

His husband.

Their first day as one.

He turned slowly, brushing a strand of hair from Gabriel's forehead. Gabriel stirred, lashes fluttering, a sleepy smile appearing.

"Good morning," he murmured, voice thick with last night's passion.

Nathan kissed him softly. "Good morning, husband."

Gabriel's smile deepened — a look of wonder crossing his face. "That's never going to get old."

Nathan nodded, cheeks warming. "Not ever."

They lay there a moment longer, wrapped in blankets and the quiet aftermath of the most epic, seismic, magical wedding the Enchanted Realm had ever seen — one that would go down in history as *the* union of two princes whose love moved the very air around them.

Meanwhile, across the house, Tyler was fully awake and fully in character.

He twirled in the media room, cape fluttering, crown crooked, replaying the wedding video on the giant screen.

"LOOK at that! Daddy's lifting Papa Nathan! NO — WAIT — THEY'RE FLOATING! OH MY—"

He leapt onto the couch, reenacting it with dramatic flair.

"My dads are so cool."

He whispered it reverently, like a secret spell.

But it *was* a secret.

He knew what his parents had told him after the ceremony:

"No telling anyone about the powers. Not yet, sweetheart."

Tyler took that seriously.

He zipped his lips, pantomimed locking the imaginary key, and threw it away.

But he *could* relive it as much as he wanted.

And he did — replaying the moment Nathan spun above the guests, the amulets glowing, the kiss that made everyone gasp.

He sighed dreamily.

"Best… day… ever…"

He only wished one thing — that Uncle Goldberg could have been there.

Tyler wasn't sure why he missed the wedding. The grown-ups said something vague about "business" and "missions."

But Tyler would learn later that Goldberg's mission had everything to do with his family.

For now, he just held the popcorn bowl over his head and shouted:

"AND THE PRINCES LIVED HAPPILY EVER AFT— AHHH!"

Tyler nearly launched off the couch as Hailey walked in wearing pajama shorts, a loose t-shirt, and freshly-brushed hair that somehow still sparkled with residual stardust.

"Chill, boy," she said, yawning as she flopped into the armchair. "You'll wake the rents."

"Hailey!" Tyler practically swooned. "What was YOUR favorite part of yesterday??"

"Oh, easy," she said, waving her hand. "When you T-POSED LIKE A HERO to hand them the rings. Iconic. Six stars. Legendary."

Tyler beamed. "Really?"

"Really, really," she said, ruffling his hair. "And then your dads turned into literal air acrobats? Honey — I almost fainted harder than Henrik."

Tyler giggled so hard he hiccupped.

A loud *grunt* sounded from the sofa in the corner.

Hailey, Tyler, and even the television itself turned.

Henrik sat up like a zombie rising from an ancient ruin — covered head to toe in glitter, ribbon, one stray streamer stuck to his eyebrow, and his glasses hanging off one ear.

"Coffee," he croaked. "Need. Coffee."

The coffee machine sputtered just then, steam hissing.

Henrik sniffed the air like a bloodhound. "YES. THE ELIXIR OF LIFE."

He stumbled toward the kitchen, tripping over a decorative pillow.

Hailey whispered, "He had a wild night."

Tyler whispered back, "Does he always look like that in the morning?"

Hailey: "Worse."

Henrik shouted from the kitchen: "I HEARD THAT!"

Ten minutes later, just as Hailey coaxed Tyler into a pancake he didn't need and Henrik had consumed half the coffee pot, soft footsteps approached from the hallway.

Nathan and Gabriel entered hand in hand.

Dressed casually — Nathan in soft denim and a fitted tee, Gabriel in charcoal joggers and a navy sweater — They both carried small travel cases.

Tyler blinked. "Are you going somewhere… without me?"

Gabriel knelt down. "Just for a bit, sweetheart. Our honeymoon."

Tyler's jaw dropped. "You're going to go be married… somewhere else?!"

Nathan laughed, hugging him. "Just for a little while. And we'll call you every day."

Gabriel added, "And you get Claire. And Hailey. And Henrik. You'll have more fun than we will."

Henrik raised a finger. "I will ensure fun is maintained at all times. I have spreadsheets."

Hailey rolled her eyes. "Oh yes, nothing says fun like spreadsheets."

Nathan shook his head fondly.

"We're going somewhere special," he said gently.

Gabriel's voice softened, warming with nostalgia.

"My homeland. My great-grandfather's estate has been partially renovated. The surrounding property is beautiful… It's peaceful. And it's ours alone for as long as we need."

Nathan smiled. "That sounds perfect."

Hailey clapped. "I expect pictures. And souvenirs. And possibly artifacts."

Henrik muttered, "Do not bring back cursed objects."

Gabriel and Nathan laughed.

Then came the goodbyes — hugging Tyler, hugging Claire, hugging Hailey, and even Henrik (who pretended it was painful).

And then—a black SUV driven by two of Gabriel's security team took the newlywed couple to the nearby airfield to board Gabriel's private jet.

Once they arrived, the small amount of luggage was loaded and the couple, hand in hand, boarded the sleek private jet that read *G.A.Michaels* on the side and a fierce lion head on the tail.

Gabriel whispered into Nathan's ear as the engines warmed:

"Ready, husband?"

Nathan leaned into him.

"I've been ready my whole life, but I have to say, I've never flown like this before. I'm only used to economy class. What an upgrade this is for sure."

"You are in for a treat then," Gabriel said with a wink as he removed his sunglasses and exchanged them for a glass of champagne offered by the flight attendant. Nathan waved off the sparkling and bubbly champagne and asked for iced tea. The flight attendant was prepared and brought him a small mason jar of freshly brewed iced tea just before she buckled in for take-off.

The jet lifted into the sky, leaving behind laughter, family, and the remnants of last night's magic and heading toward a quieter world where they could finally begin the first chapter of their married life.

(24) THE WHISPERING ESTATE

The jet dipped low over the countryside, weaving through soft morning mist that hovered above rolling hills. Nathan pressed his forehead to the window, mesmerized by the landscape below: sweeping fields glowing gold, rivers coiling like silver threads, and pockets of ancient forest clinging to the earth like secrets refusing to be forgotten.

Gabriel smiled softly. "Welcome to Korinthos." Korinthos – a quiet, little-known European country cradled between mountain ridges and river valleys. The kind of place people forgot about, except for those who traced their lineage back centuries. Like Gabriel.

When the estate came into view, Nathan's breath caught.

It was massive.

A sprawling stone manor perched atop a gentle rise, built in a style that blended old-world architecture with the raw, unpolished feel of something *timeless*—arched windows, moss-softened stairways, thick ivy climbing walls like emerald lace. Adjacent to the renovated wing stood the untouched ancestral structure: darker stone, shuttered windows, and a towering central spire that cut into the sky like a spear.

A place full of memories. And mysteries.

Gabriel's hand squeezed his.

"Welcome," he murmured again. "To where it all began."

The jet touched down on the private airstrip, and warm air enveloped them the moment they stepped out. It felt different here—thicker, charged, humming beneath the skin.

Nathan inhaled sharply.

"It feels… alive."

Gabriel nodded slowly. "It does that. We're close enough to the equator that the geomagnetic fields are stronger. My great-grandfather used to say certain places on Earth were 'thin,' where energy could pass between realms, and they amplified….everything."

Nathan's amulet pulsed once against his chest. Gabriel's glowed faintly in response.

They looked at each other.

"Even anomalies?" Nathan asked. Gabriel nodded. Nathan's heartbeat quickened.

The power had increased again. "I can feel the intensity of the amulets pulsing stronger here. I feel energy, I feel hope, I feel more alive, and I feel strong." Nathan said, and Gabriel nodded again.

And something—distant, slow, ancient—seemed to stir beneath the earth, like a creature rolling over in its sleep.

The renovated side of the manor was breathtakingly serene: high ceilings, soft linens, warm sunlight flowing through tall windows, a balcony overlooking the valley, and a stone bath fed by a natural spring.

Gabriel set down their bags and wrapped an arm around Nathan from behind.

"Thought we could start our honeymoon here," he whispered. "Just you and me. Quiet. Safe."

Nathan leaned into him.

"I love it. It feels like breathing after holding my breath too long."

But as Gabriel kissed the side of his neck, Nathan felt a pull— a tug low in his chest.

He turned his head slightly.

Toward the old wing. The untouched part of the estate.

Dark. Silent. Untamed.

Gabriel sensed it immediately.

"You feel it too."

Nathan swallowed. "It's like… something is calling."

Gabriel rested his forehead gently against Nathan's temple.

"We'll explore it. But gently. And with me leading. It's my family's history."

Nathan nodded. "Of course. I won't tear shit up so soon after marrying you. I'll follow you always."

But the amulets seemed to disagree—glowing as if eager to illuminate whatever mysteries waited within those ancient walls.

They ventured into the untouched sections late in the afternoon, when sunlight filtered through broken shutters in thin golden lines.

Dust motes danced around them. The air was colder here. Heavier.

Nathan's fingertips brushed carved doorframes, worn marble, old tapestries depicting constellations and figures in robes holding glowing orbs.

"What… exactly did your ancestors study?" Nathan whispered.

Gabriel shook his head slowly.

"My great-grandfather was always vague. He believed knowledge should be earned, not given."

Nathan paused. "Archaeology, astronomy, geomancy… Gabriel, these tapestries show the same kind of artifact shapes as the anomalies."

Gabriel's jaw tightened. "I know."

They entered a long hall lined with portraits—stern, intelligent faces watching them in stillness.

But one portrait, at the very end, made Nathan stop cold.

Gabriel's great-grandfather.

Tall. Sharp-eyed. Holding an amulet that looked *exactly like theirs.*

Nathan stepped closer.

"This can't be a coincidence."

Gabriel exhaled, voice tight with tension.

"It isn't. My family's bloodline was tied to the anomalies long before either of us was born."

Nathan turned to him slowly.

"And the anomalies chose *us*… Why?"

Gabriel met his gaze.

"That's exactly what I want to find out."

The amulets pulsed at the same moment. The air shifted.

The floor vibrated, faint but certain.

Like something— or someone— had just awakened.

That night, as they settled into the renovated suite, the truth became undeniable:

Their powers were changing.

Nathan reached to turn off a lamp—but accidentally froze the room for three full seconds instead. When time restarted, the lamp shattered into harmless glittering dust.

Gabriel attempted to pick up his mug— It shot into his hand so fast that the air cracked.

They stared at each other.

"We're stronger here," Nathan whispered.

Gabriel nodded. "Much stronger."

Nathan, breathless: "What does that mean?"

Gabriel, low voice: "It means this estate isn't just a home. It's a catalyst. We MUST be careful."

Back home, Tyler replayed the wedding video for the seventeenth time — swirling around the sofa in his cape, reenacting every magical moment while Hailey baked pancakes and Claire answered emails, Tyler dug through old shelves in the study.

He wasn't snooping. Not *really.*

But something had been bothering him all morning.

Uncle Goldberg.

Why wasn't he at the wedding?

He rummaged deeper, finding a dusty set of folders. One slid open.

Tyler froze.

Inside was a photograph:

Goldberg standing beside a government seal, Tyler didn't recognize… with Gabriel's great-grandfather visible behind him— younger, but unmistakable.

Tyler's heart hammered.

"What the…"

He dug deeper—pulling out a handwritten letter on aged parchment, sealed with the same insignia as the amulets.

As he slowly unfolded it, the words at the top made his eyes widen.

"To the guardian designated for the Bloodline's Chosen — Your mission begins now."

Tyler whispered:

"Uncle Goldberg… What are you protecting them from?"

He blinked hard, chest tightening. Was something happening to his dads?

He pressed the letter to his chest.

"I don't want to lose them," he whispered. "Not ever."

Nathan and Gabriel lay curled together that night, warm and safe in each other's arms, the moonlight spilling across their skin.

But just as sleep was beginning to claim them—

Nathan heard it.

Faint. Soft. Coming from the old wing.

A whisper.

A name.

His name.

"Nathan…"

He bolted upright. Gabriel did too.

"You heard it." Nathan's heart pounded. "Yes."

Gabriel placed a steadying hand over Nathan's, his thumb tracing calming circles.

"Tomorrow," he whispered. "We go back in. Together."

Nathan nodded.

Something in the estate wanted them. Needed them.

And whatever it was— It was ancient. It was awake. And it was watching.

(25) THE BLOODLINE AWAKENS

Morning came like a cautious visitor.

Light crept gingerly across the floorboards of the honeymoon suite, pausing at the edge of the bed as if uncertain whether it was welcome. Nathan lay on his side facing the balcony doors, watching dust drift through the beam of sunlight cutting across the room. The night's whisper still clung to him.

His name—carried through stone.

"Nathan…"

He hadn't dreamed that. Gabriel had heard it, too.

Behind him, Gabriel shifted closer, an arm sliding around his waist, the familiar weight of him pressing gently against Nathan's back.

"You're awake," Gabriel murmured, voice husky with sleep.

"Yeah." Nathan rubbed his thumb over Gabriel's knuckles. "Not sure I really slept."

"Because of the voice."

"Because of the *walls*," Nathan corrected softly. "They feel like they're listening."

Gabriel's breath hovered at the nape of his neck, warm and steady.

"They always have," he said quietly.

Nathan turned to face him.

"What do you mean, 'they always have'?"

Gabriel held his gaze for a moment too long. There was a flicker there—something like recognition, something like guilt.

"It's time you knew more," he said.

Nathan's chest tightened—not from fear, exactly, but from that electric anticipation he always felt just before the ground changed under his feet.

"Then let's go find out," he said.

The untouched ancestral wing of the Korinthos estate felt like crossing out of the present and into a held breath.

One step past the threshold, and the air changed. The temperature dropped a few degrees, but it wasn't just cold—it was dense. Heavy. Nathan felt pressure in his ears like the moment before a storm. His amulet warmed, pressing against his chest with a faint, insistent pulse.

Symbols carved into the stone archway glimmered faintly as they passed. The carvings were worn, but the shapes were achingly familiar: spirals, intersecting rings, angular sigils that echoed the geometry of the anomalies.

Nathan brushed his fingers over one symbol, and something flashed behind his eyes.

For just an instant, he saw someone else's hand—older, tanned, calloused—tracing the same lines. The vision came with the ghost-scent of ink and old leather, and a voice murmuring in another language, a prayer or formula he didn't quite understand.

He pulled his hand back, breathing a little faster.

"Did you see something?" Gabriel asked quietly.

"You could tell?"

"Your eyes went distant. And you stopped breathing."

Nathan exhaled shakily.

"I think I saw one of your ancestors. Just… their hand. Touching the stone like I did."

Gabriel nodded slowly, unsurprised.

"This place holds echoes," he said. "Energy doesn't just vanish. It settles. Especially here."

"Because of the anomalies," Nathan said.

"And because of my family," Gabriel answered.

The corridor opened into a long hall lined with portraits, each framed in dark wood, their surfaces dulled by time. Figures stared down at them—stern men, observant women, eyes painted in meticulous detail, each gaze following them no matter where they moved.

Nathan walked slowly, his footsteps sounding too loud on the stone floor.

"Who are they?" he asked.

"Direct ancestors," Gabriel said. "Every generation that held the estate. Every generation told the same stories."

"What stories?" Nathan pressed.

"Stories about a pact," Gabriel replied. "About guardians from beyond our world who chose this land as a… hinge."

"A hinge?" Nathan repeated. "Like a door hinge?"

Gabriel nodded. "A hinge between states. Between what is and what could be let in, if someone opened it."

The further they went, the more Nathan felt it—a low vibration in his bones, as if a faint engine was idling somewhere far beneath his feet.

He stopped at a portrait of a woman with tired eyes and a resolute jaw.

As he stared, his amulet flared softly, and the hall fell away.

For half a heartbeat, he saw her moving—saw her standing at a high window, rain lashing the glass, holding a small child wrapped in cloth. She whispered something into the child's hair, words full of warning and fierce love. Nathan felt the pounding fear in her chest—not fear of enemies outside, but fear of *what slept underneath*.

Then it was gone.

Nathan grasped the frame, steadying himself.

"Nathan?" Gabriel said quietly. "You with me?"

"Yeah," Nathan breathed. "I saw… one of them. A woman. Holding a baby. Afraid of what's under this place. Not of people."

Gabriel's jaw tightened.

"That tracks," he murmured.

"With what?"

He didn't answer.

Not yet.

They continued down the hall until they reached the final painting.

Gabriel's great-grandfather stared out from the last canvas like he might step down from it any moment.

He looked like an older, more severe version of Gabriel—same sharp cheekbones, same deep-set eyes, same intensity. In his painted hand, resting against his chest, was an amulet. Almost identical to the one now pressed between Nathan and Gabriel when they embraced.

Nathan's skin prickled.

"He had it," Nathan whispered. "The same kind of connection we do."

"Not the same," Gabriel said. "But close enough."

The air rippled.

That's the only way Nathan could describe it. For a split second, the hall warped at the edges, as if the world itself had taken a breath and decided not to exhale.

An image tore through his mind—too fast, too bright:

Gabriel's great-grandfather standing in a low-lit chamber, hand extended toward a shimmering anomaly fragment hovering above an altar. His eyes were wet. His voice broke on the words, *"We can't hold it forever."* Behind him, other figures argued— their voices layered and distorted, panic threaded through every syllable.

Then silence.

Nathan wrapped an arm around his middle.

"This place," he said hoarsely. "It's saturated with them. With all of them. Your whole line."

Gabriel's eyes remained fixed on the painting.

"My family believed," he said slowly, "that this land was chosen long before we were. That Korinthos was a convergence point, and the anomalies… took interest."

"'Took interest' sounds a lot like 'started experimenting,'" Nathan said.

Gabriel huffed a breath that wasn't quite a laugh.

"Maybe. Or maybe they were looking for help."

"Help with what?"

"At first?" Gabriel said. "Just stabilizing their presence here. But then something else was discovered underneath the estate. Something that made them wary."

Nathan's stomach dropped.

"Wary?"

Gabriel finally turned to face him.

"Nathan. There is something buried under this house that the anomalies didn't put here. They found it. And they were afraid of it."

"And your family decided to build on top of it," Nathan said, incredulous.

Gabriel's lips twitched in a humorless smile.

"Humans are good at that."

Nathan almost smiled back.

Almost.

"Gabriel," he said quietly. "What haven't you told me?"

Gabriel looked back up at the portrait.

And then he began.

"There's a prophecy," Gabriel said. "Passed down quietly, never written plainly, only recited to the next of kin once they were old enough not to repeat it at dinner parties."

Nathan snorted weakly. "Comforting."

Gabriel nodded.

"It always sounded like a myth to me. Until I met you."

"Go on," Nathan said.

Gabriel took a slow breath.

"When the blood of Korinthos binds with a heart from distant fire, and the sky-guardians mark them both. The sleeping bridge below shall stir.

If opened in fear, it will devour.

If opened in love, it will decide."

Nathan stared at him.

"So let me get this straight. You're the blood. I'm the 'distant fire' heart. The anomalies 'marked us both'—" he gestured to their amulet— "and now the 'sleeping bridge' is... what? Stretching? Yawning? Checking its calendar?"

Gabriel almost smiled.

"Something like that."

"And your family never thought to tell you that maybe bonding with someone from somewhere else might trigger an underground eldritch... *thing*?"

"I never believed it was more than a metaphor," Gabriel said. "A caution. A way to remind the family that we were tied to the anomalies and the land."

He glanced at the floor.

"Then the anomalies crashed into your city. You touched them. They... *chose* you."

"And then I chose you," Nathan said softly.

Gabriel nodded.

"And that's when everything in the estate started humming again. Weak at first. Then stronger. My great-grandfather used to say the Bridge was dormant, not dead. That it was waiting for *a combination* it recognized."

Nathan's throat felt dry.

"And that combination is us."

"Looks that way," Gabriel said quietly.

The amulet thumped once against Nathan's chest.

A deep vibration rolled through the hall.

Hairline cracks of light spread along the stone behind the portrait, tracing the outline of a concealed door. Dust rained from the ceiling as the wall groaned and began to shift.

Nathan stepped back, instinctively reaching for Gabriel's hand.

Beneath the grinding stone, he heard something else:

Whispers. Not directed at him, not in any language he knew, but layered and old fragments of voices from every echo that had ever seeped into this place.

The wall slid aside, revealing a stone stairway spiraling downward.

Cold air spilled out, carrying the scent of damp rock, iron, and the faint tang of ozone—like the atmosphere around the anomalies when they first arrived.

Nathan swallowed.

"We don't have to go in," he whispered, even though some part of him already knew they would.

"Yes," Gabriel said gently. "We do."

They descended together.

Every few steps, a torch flickered to life on the wall, igniting with a soft, blue-white flame that cast flickering shadows along the stone. Their amulet glowed in sympathetic pulses.

Nathan's mind flashed, unbidden, through his own life:

- The time as a child when he fell from a high tree and *should* have broken his arm, but time seemed to thicken around him, and he landed softer than he should have.
- The near car crash in college when every sound slowed, every motion stretched, and he had just enough time to turn the wheel.
- The moment at the fountain when the anomaly crashed, and everyone else screamed, but something inside him went still.

He had always written those off as luck. Adrenaline. Little miracles.

Now he wasn't so sure.

Maybe I was always being nudged, he thought. *Guided toward this.*

A shiver ran through him that had nothing to do with the temperature.

The staircase opened into a circular chamber carved directly into the rock.

Everything here had the feeling of being *deliberate*.

Shelves lined the walls, crammed with leather-bound books and scrolls tied in ribbon, their edges browned with age. Freestanding metal frames held what looked like glass cylinders—inside, faintly glowing fragments of anomaly matter floated, suspended, flickering gently like sleeping fireflies.

The floor was engraved with intricate patterns, lines, and circles intersecting in ways that made Nathan's eyes ache if he stared too long.

At the far end, raised on a dais, stood a stone altar. The symbol carved into its front matched their merged amulet exactly, down to the smallest pattern.

Nathan stepped toward it slowly, as if his body moved on its own.

The closer he got, the more his amulet hummed.

Gabriel's voice sounded far away.

"My great-grandfather used to come down here when I was a kid," he murmured. "He'd tell me that one day, someone from outside Korinthos would come. Someone whose presence made this place… shift."

Nathan glanced back at him.

"What did you think he meant?"

"I thought it was a fairy tale," Gabriel said. "A way to make me feel like my life wasn't just about old stone and family secrets."

He gestured around.

"Turns out, it was about old stone and family secrets."

Nathan almost smiled.

Then he reached the altar.

His fingertips brushed the carved symbol.

The chamber answered.

Light surged along the lines etched into the floor, racing outward in perfect symmetry. The glow climbed the walls, wove through the shelves, flashed across the anomaly fragments in the glass tubes—

—and then plunged downward, through cracks in the stone, into the earth beneath.

Nathan gasped.

He felt it.

Not just heard. Not just sensed.

Felt it.

Something far below shifted in response. Something massive. Something old.

It was like feeling an enormous creature twitch in its sleep under the foundation of the world.

"Gabriel," Nathan whispered. "What is *under* us?"

Gabriel's face was pale, eyes wide.

"My family called it the Bridge," he said. "They believed it was a construct—or a being, or both—that could open pathways between realms. The anomalies didn't create it. They found it. Then they made a pact with my family to keep it from waking in the wrong hands."

"In the wrong hands," Nathan repeated. "So, it's dangerous."

"In the wrong *intent*," Gabriel corrected. "The prophecy says if the Bridge opens in fear, it will devour. If it opens in love, it will decide."

"Decide *what*?" Nathan asked.

Gabriel's silence was answer enough.

Their amulet pulsed a second time.

The floor trembled.

This time, loose dust fell from the ceiling in soft streams. A low sound rose from beneath the earth—too low to be a voice, but carrying the feel of one. Not words, but sensation:

HUNGRY.

WAITING.

CHOSEN.

Nathan staggered back from the altar.

"I don't think it cares about our schedules," he said shakily.

"No," Gabriel agreed, voice grim. "It doesn't."

In the study back home, the quiet felt heavy, like the pause before a thunderclap.

Tyler sat at the desk with the letter spread out in front of him. The first page explained the guardianship role Goldberg had accepted. The second page… he hadn't read until now.

His hands trembled slightly as he smoothed it flat.

Hailey perched on the edge of the desk, not joking for once. Claire stood nearby, arms crossed tightly, as if holding herself together.

"Read it out loud if you can," Claire said gently. "We're here."

Tyler swallowed.

His voice shook as he read:

*"To the guardian appointed:

When the anomalies merge and select their bearers, and the bloodline of Korinthos and the foreign heart of fire are bound, the Bridge beneath Korinthos will begin to stir.

173

When it does, they will not be alone in knowing. Others—those who hunger for crossing and conquest—will feel it too. They will seek the Chosen, hoping to use them as keys.

Your mission: protect them from those who would force the Bridge open in fear or greed.

If you fail, the worlds will bleed."*

Tyler's voice cracked on the last line.

He looked up, eyes wide and wet.

"Uncle Goldberg is protecting Dad and Papa Nathan from people who want to use them," he whispered. "From people who want to make them open something terrible."

Claire's face had gone pale. Hailey rubbed Tyler's back, her hand small but steady.

"And the Bridge is under where they're staying," Tyler added, voice breaking. "They're there. And it's waking up. And those bad people will know."

Claire's phone showed *No Signal* for the third time.

Hailey muttered, "Of course. Of course, the creepy underground thing is messing with communications."

Tyler clenched his fists around the letter.

"I don't want to lose them," he said. "Not my dad. Not my Papa Nathan. I *just* got them. I don't want this stupid Bridge, or these people, or anything else to take them away."

Claire pulled him into her arms and held on fiercely.

"We're going to figure this out," she murmured. "Goldberg is out there for a reason. Your dads are strong. And they have each other."

Tyler pressed his face into her shoulder, tears hot and silent.

He didn't know that miles away, underground in Korinthos, the same energy that made his chest ache was now blooming under his father's feet, answering the presence of their joined amulet like a long-awaited call.

In the vault below the estate, the light along the floor dimmed, but the sensation didn't.

It intensified.

Nathan staggered, bracing a hand on the wall.

Images pressed into his mind—too fast to fully grasp, but leaving impressions:

- A night sky torn by shimmering fissures.
- A river that flowed upward into the stars.
- Shapes moving on the other side of a translucent veil.
- A pair of hands—someone's, maybe his, maybe not—resting on a surface that felt like stone and thunder at the same time.

He gasped and clutched his head.

"Nathan," Gabriel said sharply, moving to him. "Talk to me. What are you seeing?"

"I don't know," Nathan panted. "Doors. Or not doors. Rips. Something that wants to open. And… and something that wants *through*."

He forced himself to breathe, to push the images back enough to speak.

"This Bridge," he said hoarsely, "it's not just a thing. It's a… will. It wants a say. It wants to… *decide* the way the prophecy said."

Gabriel nodded grimly.

"And it wants to decide through us," he said. "Through what we choose. Through how we feel when we face it."

A cold dread slid into Nathan's gut.

"So, if we're afraid, it devours. If we meet it in love, it… what? Sorts? Judges? Picks a path?"

"Or closes itself again," Gabriel said softly. "For centuries. Maybe longer."

"And meanwhile," Nathan said slowly, "others—whoever Goldberg is fighting—will know it's waking. They'll be coming. They'll see us as walking keys."

He looked up at Gabriel, heart pounding.

"Do you still think we're on a honeymoon?"

Gabriel huffed out a breath that wasn't quite a laugh.

"No," he said. "I think we're standing on top of a choice my family's been avoiding for generations."

The ground pulsed once more.

The Bridge, whatever it was, had felt them.

It knew they were there.

And it was waiting.

(26) THE FIRE THAT ANSWERS

At first, Nathan thought it was another tremor.

The floor shivered, the air warped a fraction, and the torches along the chamber walls bowed inward as if something enormous had just inhaled beneath the rock.

But this wasn't like before.

Before, the estate had *vibrated*. Now, it *tilted*—subtly, impossibly, as if the world had turned its face toward him.

"Nathan?"

Gabriel's voice sounded close and far at the same time.

Nathan meant to turn his head toward him. Meant to say, *I'm okay, I'm fine,* meant to make some useless joke to lighten the pressure in his chest.

Instead, reality cut sideways.

The chamber fell away like a sheet being pulled from a table. The stone, the torches, the altar, all folded out of existence—and for a breathless instant, Nathan existed in nothing but a rush of soundless white.

Then… not-white.

Not any color he had words for.

He was standing—if this counted as standing—on something that behaved like a surface but looked like a sky. Beneath his feet, patterns of light flickered and rearranged themselves, like constellations being redrawn in real time. Above him, threads of brilliance stretched out in every direction, intersecting, weaving, pulsing in rhythms that made his teeth ache.

There was no air, but he could breathe.

There was no up or down, but he knew instinctively where *below* was.

And *below* was watching him.

A presence gathered itself like a storm. Not in one place, but everywhere. In the shimmer, in the threads, in the vibrational hum that thrummed through his bones.

When it spoke, it didn't use words.

It pressed *meaning* into him like a hand against his sternum.

Welcome, Foreign Fire.

Nathan flinched.

He'd expected something cruel, alien, jagged. Something so far removed from anything human that he could blame every cold thing in the universe on it.

Instead, what he felt was… old.

Old and vast and immeasurably tired.

Who are you? Nathan thought—or maybe whispered. It was hard to tell where his mouth ended, and his mind began in this place. *Are you the Bridge?*

The entity's response carried a strange, layered texture, like a thousand echoes agreeing at once.

I am the Mind that remains. The Structure sleeps in stone. The Path is what the anomalies built. Together, they called us the Bridge.

Images flooded Nathan's senses, not sequential, but overlapping:

A sphere of stone and crystal, buried deep beneath the estate, wrapped in bands of light. Winged beings—anomalies in their true forms—circling it at a distance, weaving threads through its surface with gentle precision. Gabriel's great-grandfather is placing his hands on an altar, eyes hollow with responsibility. An entire bloodline swearing themselves to something they never fully understood.

Nathan staggered, bare feet slipping on not-ground.

Slow down, he thought, gasping. *You're showing me too much—*

The presence softened.

Your structure was not made for this, Foreign Fire. You are small. A pause. And yet… not.

Nathan's chest tightened; instinctive annoyance flared.

"Small is relative," he said—this time actually hearing his own voice. It sounded thin but steady in the endless in-between.

The Bridge—entity—whatever it was—considered that.

Small bodies. Large consequences.

The threads around him brightened, lines of light turning, folding, knotting themselves into a shape that almost resembled… a hand.

A question pressed into him like a probe.

(What are you?)

Nathan swallowed.

"I'm Nathan. I'm… human."

No.

The answer came so quickly it knocked the breath from him.

You are *partly* what you say. But your flame is older than your flesh. It does not belong to the anomalies. It does not belong to this world. It does not belong to me.

Nathan's pulse stuttered.

Older than my flesh…?

Memories surfaced in jagged flashes:

The fall from the tree at eight years old, when everything slowed, and he landed as if something had cushioned him midair. The night in high school when the car ahead of him spun out and time stretched just enough for him to steer around it, margins so tight it should've been impossible. The way his skin tingled the first time the anomaly had appeared at the fountain—how the world had gone perfectly silent for him while everyone else screamed.

He'd always chalked those moments up to luck.

"Then what *am* I?" he whispered.

The threads around him pulsed.

A convergence. A spark born where many lines meet. A flame that is not bound.

The voice shifted subtly—not its size, but its *posture*.

As if it were bracing itself.

You could unmake me, Nathan.

The words rang in his bones.

He stared into the impossible distance, into the vast intelligence that wrapped around him like a nebula.

"That's… not what I want," he said slowly. "Why would I destroy you?"

Want and capacity are not the same. For the first time, a note crept into the entity's tone that Nathan recognized intimately.

Fear.

I was raised from the anomalies' essence. Shaped to anchor pathways between worlds. But the force in you does not match their design. It is wild. It is—

The next concept came with no perfect translation. The closest word Nathan's mind reached for was *unwritten.*

Unwritten, the entity agreed. You are a line the story has not planned.

Nathan's mouth went dry.

"I didn't ask for that," he said. "I never wanted to be some… cosmic glitch."

You are not a glitch. You are a choice.

The entity's attention sharpened, focusing on him so completely he felt flayed and held all at once.

You chose the bloodline bearer. You chose the child. You chose love where others chose power. That is why you terrify me.

Nathan's breath shuddered.

Images flashed again—not given by the entity this time, but pulled from his own memory:

Gabriel was asleep on his shoulder after a twenty-hour workday, lines of exhaustion smoothed out by trust. Tyler's fingers curling in his shirt the night he'd asked, *Will you leave if I do something wrong?* The way his own voice had shaken when he'd told the kid he was staying, even if he wasn't sure the universe would let him.

He squared his shoulders.

"I'm not leaving them," he said. "I don't care what you are or what you want or what anyone else thinks should happen down here. They're mine. My family. I stand with them."

The void thrummed.

The threads convulsed, flaring so bright they bordered on painful.

Yes. The entity's thought-voice came lower, almost hoarse. This is what I feared.

The lights around him shifted again.

Now Nathan saw three strands of brilliance—one gold, one deep blue, one fire-white—twining together in a loose spiral.

The gold line split briefly into two at one end, forming a smaller offshoot that nonetheless remained woven tightly into the others.

Images layered over it:

Gabriel Nathan Tyler

I have watched centuries of bearers, the entity said. Bloodline guardians. Cowards. Martyrs. Users. None like this.

The three threads pulsed.

This pattern…*family*… should not exist with the power of this scale. It was never designed for love. It was designed for control.

Nathan's jaw clenched.

"Then maybe the design was wrong."

Silence.

For the first time since he arrived in this impossible place, the hum receded. Not completely, but like a held breath easing.

You alter the equation, Foreign Fire. Through you, this Bridge may judge differently. Through you, it may refuse to open. Or open only to some. Or close forever. I cannot see beyond your choices.

Nathan took that in slowly.

"You kept saying 'they' will come," he said. "Who are they?"

The void dimmed.

Those who feed on crossing. Those who would shatter worlds for the thrill of walking between them. Those whose scent awakens and follow it like sharks follow blood. They are already near. Your guardian holds them at bay.

"Goldberg," Nathan breathed.

Images washed over him—this time not abstract: Branches whipping by. Gunfire cracking trees. A massive figure—Goldberg—slamming someone into the earth, a sigil burned into their wrist that matched *none* of the anomaly markings, but something darker, hungrier.

Goldberg was shouting into comms that weren't working. Goldberg gritting his teeth, muttering, *You're not touching my kids. Not today.*

Nathan's stomach lurched.

He's out there alone.

Not alone, the entity corrected. Aligned. The anomalies mark him as an extension. He fights in tandem with their will.

Nathan felt his eyes sting.

"I can't help him from here," he whispered.

You can help by choosing well. The entity's presence leaned closer again. Everything in your life has led you to this convergence. Your flame. Your love. Your defiance. The Bridge will not make the choice for you. It will reflect your heart and amplify it. If you come to it in fear, it will consume. If you come to it in love—truly, wholly—it may unmake those who approach with greed. Including me.

Nathan's chest ached.

"You're afraid I'll kill you by loving too hard?" he asked, half-broken, half-incredulous.

A pause.

Yes.

He almost laughed.

"If that's the risk, then you know who I'm choosing," he whispered. "And it's not you."

The void shuddered.

But beneath the fear, Nathan sensed something else rising through the entity—a tiny, reluctant ember of… respect.

Then I must prepare, the Bridge said. For my end. Or my transformation.

The place began to thin at the edges, the star-threads blurring into soft streaks of light.

Nathan realized, distantly, that he was being pushed back—lifted—returned.

"Nathan."

A hand, warm and rough and real, grasped his.

He heard his name again—not from the Bridge this time.

From Gabriel.

He gasped awake on stone, lungs sucking in damp air that smelled like dust and old energy.

The chamber roared back into place—the shelves, the glass tubes, the glowing floor patterns—all slightly too sharp, like someone had turned the contrast up on reality.

Gabriel crouched over him, one hand braced on his chest, the other holding tightly to his fingers.

"Nathan. Hey. Look at me."

Nathan forced his eyes to focus.

Gabriel's face appeared above him—worried, exhausted, impossibly dear.

"You were out," Gabriel said, voice tight. "You just… stopped. You went stiff, and then you weren't *here*. I couldn't—"

He broke off, jaw working.

Nathan tightened his hand around Gabriel's.

"I was with it," he rasped. "With the Bridge."

Gabriel's fingers flexed.

"Did it hurt you?"

Nathan thought of the fear he'd felt vibrating through a thing older than any empire on Earth.

"Not exactly," he said. "It… welcomed me. Sort of. It called me the Foreign Fire. Said I could unmake it. Or open it forever."

Gabriel inhaled sharply, eyes darkening.

"That tracks with what my great-grandfather feared," he muttered. "He thought one day someone would come along who could end this stand-off entirely. He just didn't think they'd be you."

Nathan swallowed.

"It's scared, Gabriel," he whispered. "Not just of people who want to use it. Of *me*. Because it can't see past what I might do if I choose love over fear."

Gabriel's expression shifted.

"Of course you'd terrify a reality anchor," he said, trying to smile through the anxiety. "You terrify me sometimes."

Nathan managed a ragged laugh.

"Good."

Gabriel's gaze softened.

"Did it say anything about the ones coming after us?"

"Yeah," Nathan said quietly. "It said they're already near. And Goldberg is… fighting them off. Somehow, he's working with the anomalies. They've marked him as… an extension."

Gabriel swore under his breath, eyes shining with gratitude and guilt.

"Of course he is," he whispered. "He promised me he'd keep us clear long enough to figure this out."

Nathan squeezed his hand.

"We're not alone," he said. "Even when it feels like it."

Gabriel looked at him like he wanted to memorize his face all over again.

"You went in alone," he said. "Don't do that again."

Nathan's answer came without hesitation.

"Then don't let go."

On the other side of the world, Tyler sat on the floor of the media room, wedding video paused on a frame of his two dads suspended midair in their first kiss as husbands.

He was trying very hard not to cry.

They looked so powerful there. So untouchable. So… *theirs.*

But the letter with Goldberg's warning lay open beside him, and it made his stomach twist every time he looked at the words *if you fail, the worlds will bleed.*

He pressed the heels of his hands to his eyes.

"Please be okay," he whispered into the darkness. "Please, please be okay."

Then— a soundless click.

Like a radio channel changing in his head.

And a voice, familiar and warm, slid into his thoughts like light through a crack in a door.

Tyler?

Tyler jerked upright.

"Dad?"

It's me. Gabriel's presence was steady, like a hand between his shoulder blades. *I don't have long. The estate interferes with a lot. But we found a… channel.*

"Are you okay?" Tyler blurted out. "Is Papa Nathan okay? Is everyone okay—"

Hey. Breathe, little prince. Gabriel's reassurance wrapped around him, soothing his racing heart. *We're alive. We're together. That's the most important thing.*

Tyler swallowed, eyes burning.

"What's happening? What's under the house? Is it bad? Is it gonna hurt you?"

A pause.

It's not simple, Gabriel admitted. *There's something old and powerful beneath us. And some very bad people are trying to find their way here. Goldberg is keeping them busy.*

Tyler's voice cracked.

"Uncle Goldberg *is* okay, right?"

For now, Gabriel said. No one is better suited to handle a fight than him. You know how he is.

Tyler could almost see Goldberg rolling his shoulders like a bull ready to charge.

"What can I do?" Tyler whispered. "I'm all the way over here. I can't help."

You can. Gabriel's tone shifted—gentle but firm. Listen carefully. Things might get… weird for you soon. You might see images, hear voices in your mind that don't sound like your own. That's how some of these entities and people try to get in. To scare you. To trick you.

Tyler's fingers tightened around the edge of the couch.

"What do I do?"

If it's not Papa Nathan, Gabriel said, shut it out. Don't talk back to it. Don't argue. Just imagine slamming a door in its face. Over and over again. We'll feel the pressure from here. We'll know.

Tyler nodded quickly, even though he knew his dad couldn't see him.

"O-okay. I can do that. I promise. I'll keep the doors shut."

A warmth pulsed through him at that—like Gabriel's amulet had just flickered inside his ribcage.

That's my brave boy, Gabriel said softly. And listen—

He hesitated.

Tyler's breath caught.

When we come home… Papa Nathan might seem a little different.

Tyler's heart squeezed.

"Different how? Is he… is he gonna be scary?"

No. Gabriel's answer was immediate, unwavering. Never to you. He's touched something powerful. It's changing him, but in ways that are *good.* Like a light getting brighter. It might make people around him uncomfortable at first. But not us.

Tyler swallowed.

"So I… I should… Should I help him?"

You already do, Gabriel replied. Just love him. Accept him. Remind him he's yours. His power is big, but his heart is still the same. Your Papa is still your hero. Just—maybe one who glows.

A watery laugh forced its way out of Tyler.

"Superhero glow," he whispered.

Exactly. A faint whisper of a smile colored Gabriel's tone. We'll be back as soon as we can. Until then, listen to Mom, Hailey, and Henrik. And Tyler?

"Yeah?"

Thank you for being part of our pattern.

The connection loosened, the presence receding like a wave pulling back from shore.

"Dad? Dad—?"

Silence.

Tyler exhaled slowly. His fear was still there, but beneath it was something else now. A weight that didn't feel crushing.

A responsibility.

He laid his hand over his chest and whispered:

"I'll keep the doors shut. I promise."

In the chamber, Gabriel and Nathan leaned against each other on the stairs, halfway between the altar and the passage leading deeper underground.

Nathan's cheek rested briefly against Gabriel's shoulder. The contact steadied him; it also doubled as a reminder of everything he'd just told the Bridge.

I stand with him. Whatever happens below this house, I stand with him.

Gabriel watched the floor lines slowly dim back to their previous faint glow.

"You realize," he said quietly, "to everyone else in my family, the Bridge was mostly an obligation. A burden. At best, an emergency backup plan. No one ever considered it might have… feelings about us."

Nathan snorted softly.

"Well, congratulations. We've traumatized an ancient interdimensional lock with our relationship."

Gabriel huffed out a breath that was half-laugh, half-sob.

"Of course we did."

Nathan turned his head to look at him.

"It wasn't just afraid of me," he said, serious now. "It showed me us. You, me, and Tyler. Like strands of light. It kept focusing on that. It couldn't understand how something with this much potential to alter reality chose to build… a *family* instead of an empire."

Gabriel's eyes shone.

"Well," he said, "empires fall. Family doesn't."

Nathan nodded slowly.

"It thinks I can destroy it," he continued quietly. "But what really scares it is that I might destroy the *rules* it thought it had to live by."

Gabriel reached up and brushed his thumb across Nathan's lower lip, as if reassuring himself he was really there.

"I don't care how scared it is," he said. "I'm more afraid of losing you. Or Tyler. Or myself. So, whatever choices we make down there? We make them together. No self-sacrificing nonsense. No noble death speeches. You hear me?"

Nathan's throat tightened.

"I hear you," he whispered.

The amulet between them warmed, pulsing once.

The passage leading deeper into the earth loomed before them—a dark throat in the rock, whispering with distant power.

Nathan straightened.

"Ready?" he asked.

Gabriel stood too.

"Terrified," he answered. Then smiled. "Which is why I'm glad I'm doing this with you."

They turned toward the darkness.

Above them, the ancestral estate watched with stone eyes and silent portraits.

Below them, the Bridge waited—afraid and hopeful and utterly unprepared for the love walking toward it.

And somewhere in the forests of Korinthos, Bill Goldberg wiped blood from his lip, squared his shoulders against the line of enemy combatants forming in front of him, and growled:

"All right, you sons of bitches. You want my family?"

He cracked his neck.

"Come earn it."

The worlds, seen and unseen, held their breath.

The Foreign Fire walked deeper.

And for the first time in its ancient existence, the entity below did not know if it would survive what came next.

(27) THE ARMOR OF HEAVEN

Tyler's small hands moved fast, almost frantic, stuffing clothes, a notebook, headphones, a flashlight, and his favorite plush lion into his duffel bag. The zipper trembled under his grip as he dragged it shut.

"Tyler," Claire said gently from the doorway. "Honey… what are you doing?"

He hesitated. His shoulders rose and fell with one shaky breath.

"I just… I have to be ready."

"For what, sweetheart?"

"Dad said things might get weird," Tyler blurted, voice cracking. "He said voices could come, or pictures that aren't mine, and I have to slam the door on them. Like… in my head."

Claire slowly sat on the edge of the bed.

"You heard Gabriel in your *mind*?"

Tyler nodded. Hard.

"I think he and Papa Nathan are gonna need me. Maybe not right now, but soon. And what if we have to go to them? Mom, please don't think I'm crazy."

Her eyebrows softened, eyes glistening with a quiet understanding she couldn't articulate.

"Tyler… after what I saw at the wedding…" she murmured, "after the floating… and the lights… and the way they vanished for a moment during the vows…"

She closed her eyes. For the first time, she let herself believe this was bigger than her skepticism allowed.

"I don't think you're crazy," she whispered. "I think I'm the one who didn't want to see."

Tyler's lip trembled. He crawled into her arms and held her tight.

"When I talk to Dad…" he whispered, "it feels real. And warm. And safe."

Claire stroked his hair.

"I wish I could talk to him, too," she admitted. "Just once. To know what's happening."

Tyler pulled back, wiping his eyes.

"When he comes home," Tyler said with sudden certainty, "he's gonna need you too."

Nathan and Gabriel moved deeper into the earth, torches sparking nervously along the chamber walls as they passed. Each step took them lower than any map of the estate suggested was possible — but the architecture didn't argue.

The passage seemed almost… aware of them.

Symbols glowed faintly under the stone dust, warming as Nathan approached, dimming when Gabriel stepped forward, then flaring almost painfully bright when they walked together.

"The Bridge is sensing us," Gabriel murmured.

"No," Nathan whispered. "It's *studying* us."

Something ancient stirred inside him. Lines of Scripture he had memorized since childhood rose like water drawn from a deep well. Nathan's voice steadied, resonant, as he began to speak Psalm 23—not merely reciting it, but declaring it, as though each verse carried weight in the unseen realm.

1. The Lord is my shepherd, I shall not want.

2. He makes me lie down in green pastures; He leads me beside still waters.

3. He restores my soul; He guides me in the paths of righteousness for His name's sake.

4. Even though I walk through the valley of the shadow of death, I fear no evil, for You are with me; Your rod and Your staff, they comfort me.

5. You prepare a table before me in the presence of my enemies; You have anointed my head with oil; My cup overflows.

6. Surely goodness and lovingkindness will follow me all the days of my life, and I will dwell in the house of the Lord forever.

As the final English syllable left his lips, another current—older, deeper—rose up through him. His voice shifted, taking on a cadence he had never learned, belonging to a time far behind memory.

1. Yahweh ro'i, lo echsar.

2. Binot deshe yarbitzeini; al mei menuchot y'nahaleini.

3. Nafshi y'shovev; yancheini b'maglei-tzedek l'ma'an shemo.

4. Gam ki-elech b'gei tzalmavet, lo-ira ra ki-atah imadi— shivtecha u'mishantecha, hemah y'nachamuni.

5. Ta'aroch l'fanai shulchan neged tzor'rai; dishanta vashemen roshi, kosi revaya.

6. Ach tov v'chesed yirdefuni kol y'mei chayai; v'shavti b'veit Yahweh l'orech yamim.

Gabriel stared, awestruck. "Nathan… what language was that? It felt ancient. Beautiful."

"I—I think it was Hebrew," Nathan said, blinked, trying to steady himself. "While I spoke it, I envisioned a teenage boy… a shepherd. He reminded me of David."

"Who is David?" Gabriel asked gently.

"Oh—sorry." Nathan managed a breathy, incredulous laugh. "David's from the Old Testament. Just a shepherd boy at first… then the one who killed the giant Goliath… and later the second king of Israel. He wrote Psalm 23—about God guiding him through every danger and every storm."

Gabriel looked at him, soft and reverent. "And now it's guiding you."

The further they continued downward, the air grew denser, tinged with metallic cold, the scent of ancient iron and something older — like scorched atmosphere after a celestial battle.

Then they emerged into a vaulted chamber.

Weapons lined the walls.

Spears with obsidian tips glowing faintly from inside. Shields hammered from metals no human forge ever created. Helmets with wings etched into the sides, cracked from battles centuries old. Gauntlets still humming with the faintest residue of energy that felt like starlight trapped in metal.

Gabriel's breath hitched.

"These are… ancestral relics," he whispered. "My family told stories but… I thought they were myths."

Nathan stepped toward a sword mounted at the center of the wall. The blade looked like silver but pulsed with streaks of blue fire.

When Gabriel reached for it—

Nathan gasped.

A story slammed into him:

A battlefield under a cracked red sky. A younger ancestor of Gabriel — armor dented, one winged pauldron shattered — holding that very sword while an anomaly towered over him like a burning sun. The two clashed in a storm of light so fierce the ground split. The ancestor shouting a prayer in a language Nathan didn't know but recognized deep inside. A roar — not of rage, but devotion.

Then darkness.

Nathan stumbled back, choking on the afterimage.

Gabriel rushed to him.

"Nathan—what happened?"

"I saw him," Nathan whispered hoarsely. "Your ancestor. Fighting beside an anomaly. A war. A sky that wasn't ours. I… I watched him die."

Gabriel's breath caught.

Nathan's hands shook. His amulet burned against his chest, pulsing out of rhythm.

Then suddenly—

A voice he hadn't heard in years rose in his mind.

Not the Bridge. Not an anomaly.

But Scripture whispered in the tone his grandmother once used when comforting a frightened little boy:

"For God has not given you a spirit of fear, but of power, and of love, and of a sound mind."

Nathan froze. The words filled him with a warmth so total his knees nearly buckled.

Gabriel saw it.

"Nathan…?"

Nathan inhaled deeply. His voice steadied.

"That wasn't the Bridge," he whispered. "That was God."

The chamber brightened — first softly, Then so intensely Gabriel shielded his eyes.

Light poured down in pillars. Multiple. Seven.

Nathan stepped forward instinctively.

And the light moved with him.

The air vibrated like a song made of thunder and silk.

Then, through the light—**wings.**

Massive, incandescent wings unfurled from the pillars. Figures emerged, each one towering, blazing, radiant with a heat that didn't burn.

Gabriel gasped.

"Nathan… those are—"

"Angels," Nathan breathed.

The tallest stepped forward.

His presence bent the air.

His armor looked forged from the dawn of creation, and every feather shimmered like molten gold.

"**Nathan,**" he said, voice layered with eternity, **"I am Michael, prince of the heavenly hosts. We have known of you since before your form was woven.**"

Nathan trembled, but didn't step back.

Michael turned slightly, and the other pillars dimmed just enough to reveal the rest:

—Raphael —Uriel —Selaphiel —Jegudiel —Barachiel

And last—

A figure stepped from the light, and Gabriel froze.

He looked just like him. Exactly like him. Except radiant beyond measure.

"Gabriel," the angel said gently, bowing his head to his human counterpart. **"Namesake. Flesh of mortal, heart of lion. You are seen.**"

Human Gabriel's chest shuddered.

"Why are you here?" Nathan whispered.

Michael approached him.

"To arm you."

Light swirled, lifting dust, pebbles, and air into spiraling vortices of radiance.

"The Bridge fears you because it sees only a fraction of who you are."

Metal shaped from light appeared — transparent yet solid, like crystallized holiness.

"The Armor of God is not a metaphor," Michael said. **"It is a gift. And you — Foreign Fire — are permitted to bear it just as Nathaniel did in the olden times.**"

Gabriel blinked, stunned. "Nathaniel?" he echoed, turning to Nathan. "You're… in the Bible too?"

Before Nathan could answer, the host parted. The Archangel Gabriel — the heavenly version — stepped forward first, his eyes warm with recognition as he looked at the man who shared his name.

"Nathaniel was a prophet," he said aloud, speaking so his human counterpart could hear every word. "A messenger of God who strengthened King David in his reign. He walked in truth, and truth walked with him."

Nathan's breath caught. He didn't feel worthy — not even close. Yet something ancient tugged inside him, the echo of a lineage he knew he carried.

The Archangel Gabriel lifted his hands.

The Belt of Truth — placed by Gabriel the Archangel.

Warmth wrapped Nathan's waist, tightening with a calm certainty.

The Breastplate of Righteousness — placed by Selaphiel.

It formed over Nathan's chest like liquid light, settling into perfect clarity.

The Shoes of Peace — placed by Barachiel.

Translucent sandals appeared, glowing faintly with a soft, steady brilliance.

The Shield of Faith — forged by Jegudiel.

A barrier of pure radiance shimmered into Nathan's hand, weightless yet indestructible.

The Helmet of Salvation — placed by Raphael.

A crown-like helm descended, fitting gently, filling Nathan's mind with impossible clarity.

And finally—

The Sword of the Spirit — carried by Michael.

He knelt.

The archangel knelt before him.

"Nathan, son of God, Foreign Fire made flesh — This is the Word given form."

The sword materialized in Michael's hands, blade shimmering with every color light could imagine and several it couldn't.

"Why me?" Nathan whispered, voice broken by awe and vocalizing his unworthiness.

Michael looked up, eyes like blazing planets.

"Because love chose you."

He extended the sword.

Nathan reached out—

And the chamber detonated into white fire.

When the brilliance faded, Nathan stood in the center of the chamber—**Glowing.**

Not lightly. Not subtly.

Light poured from him in ribbons, reflections, halos— as if God Himself had reached into Nathan's ribs and whispered, *Shine.*

Gabriel could only stare.

"Nathan..." he breathed, voice breaking. "My God... what are you...?"

Nathan didn't answer—because in the stillness beneath the roar of light, a voice moved inside him. Not thunder. Not fire. But the steady, familiar warmth of the One he had loved since childhood.

"Still yours," Jesus said within him—gentle, unshakable, eternal. **"And I AM who is, and was, and forever will be— with you in the valley, and with you on the mountaintop."**

Nathan's knees nearly buckled at the sweetness of it.

All around them, the angels bowed—wings lowered, heads bent, not to Nathan but to the Presence shining through him.

The chamber trembled as though recognizing its true Sovereign.

And deep beneath their feet, the Bridge stirred— not in hostility, not in defense, but in **bewildered awe**, sensing something it had never encountered in all its unnatural existence:

Not power. Not authority. But **the nearness of the Living God** is carried inside a human frame.

A human carrying divine authority. A love powerful enough to rewrite fate. A Foreign Fire even heaven had anticipated.

Gabriel stepped forward, touching Nathan's glowing cheek, tears slipping down his face.

"I won't lose you," he whispered.

Nathan lifted the Sword of the Spirit, its blade humming.

"You won't," he said. "Because love wins."

The chamber responded— stone cracking, light bursting, the earth itself bending.

Something far below awakened— **and it knew its judge had arrived.**

(28) THE HOSTS OF THE ALMIGHTY

The chamber was still shaking when Nathan lifted the Sword of the Spirit.

Not shaking from danger. Not shaking from the Bridge. Not shaking from the anomalies.

It shook because Heaven had entered the room.

Gabriel felt the pressure in his chest shift — not heavy, not suffocating, but *reverent*—as if every molecule of air realized whose presence had been invoked.

Nathan glowed with a brilliance that made the torches flicker backward in awe.

And then—

A sound like a thousand wings unfurling at once surged through the underground.

fwshhhhhhhhhhhhh—

Not wind. Movement.

Nathan's eyes widened.

"The army…" he whispered. "The army of God is… answering."

Michael's voice thundered gently:

"The Almighty moves when His warrior calls."

A second pillar of light burst beside him, then another, then a dozen more. The angels who had armed him stepped aside, reverent, as radiant forms marched from the breach between realms:

- towers of armored light

- wings that cut through the air like living flame
- swords that hummed with scripture
- shields inscribed with psalms
- faces set in holy determination

Not one of them touched the ground. They hovered, each radiating the righteousness of a thousand dawns.

Gabriel staggered back, overwhelmed.

"Nathan… this is—"

"I know," Nathan whispered, voice full of something more than awe. Something like belonging. Something like truth long buried, finally rising.

"I am not God," Nathan said aloud— and the armies of Heaven stilled, wings folding, weapons lowered, waiting. "But I fight fiercely for Him. He is the Almighty. And in Him do I live… and move… and have my being."

At those words— at that declaration ringing with identity, humility, and truth— The entire celestial host bowed as one, a tidal wave of armor, wings, and radiant power cascading downward.

Then— from ten thousand times ten thousand throats, from dominions, thrones, powers, and blazing seraphim— a voice like the roar of creation's first dawn thundered:

"HALLELUJAH TO THE LORD ALMIGHTY!"

It rolled like oceans colliding. It shook the foundations of unseen realms. It carried the weight of galaxies and the purity of eternal fire. And the earth itself trembled beneath the sound. of Heaven giving praise to its King.

The light intensified until even Gabriel had to shield his eyes.

Michael spoke again — but this time, he addressed the entire army.

"Hear the commissioning. Hear the chosen. Hear the bearer of flame. whom God Himself has marked."

Nathan's armor ignited — the transparent plating flaming into radiance that refused to be ignored or dimmed.

Every color of light burst from him:

- gold
- violet
- white
- azure
- crimson
- sunfire
- emerald
- and shades human eyes had no name for

Gabriel stared—unable to breathe for a moment. "You're… shining," he whispered. "Nathan, you're—"

Nathan turned toward him, and the light around him softened just enough for Gabriel to feel it: warmth like sunlight, purity like fresh air after a storm, a nearness that felt unmistakably holy.

"I shine only because He shines through me," Nathan said, voice low and steady. "And today… We will witness His power in a way humanity has not seen since the apostle John stood before the glorified Christ."

Before Gabriel could speak, the atmosphere changed.

Heat rippled through the air— not burning, but commanding.

The ground beneath their feet gave a long, aching groan, as if the earth itself recognized the presence descending upon it.

And the Bridge— that ancient, defiant structure— pulsed once, twice, like something caught between terror and fury under the weight of approaching glory.

The anomalies' ancient energy recoiled and surged, confused by this new intensity.

And miles away, in the forest—

Bill Goldberg, bloodied and panting, freezing mid-punch, turned his head upward.

Trees glowed faintly in the reflection of Nathan's awakening.

Goldberg's eyes widened.

"…Well, I'll be damned," he muttered reverently. "That's my boy."

Beneath the chamber floor, deeper than stone, deeper than anomaly, deeper than time—

The Bridge stirred.

But not in its earlier hunger. Not in its earlier arrogance.

This stirring was fear.

The consciousness that had watched worlds turn felt something it had never felt — something that did not come from anomalies or bloodlines or ancient duty.

It felt Heaven touch Earth. And it trembled.

"Foreign fire…" the entity whispered into the stone. "…what are you doing?"

The entire chamber flashed — once, violently.

Nathan stepped forward, wings of light (not physical, but unmistakable) unfurling behind him.

The angels parted like a tide.

Michael lifted his sword in salute.

The archangel Gabriel bowed his head toward his human namesake.

Uriel's wings flared with anticipation.

Raphael whispered blessings of strength over Nathan's armor.

Every being in the chamber recognized it:

Nathan had become a vessel not of anomaly, not of prophecy, but of *God's authority*.

He stepped toward the passage leading deeper to the Bridge.

The ground beneath him healed as he walked. Cracks sealed. Dust lifted and vanished. Symbols once faded glowed like fire drawn by his presence.

Gabriel followed him — not behind, not beneath, but beside — because that's where love stands.

Nathan reached the threshold. The Sword of the Spirit sparked with holy electricity.

He turned to Gabriel.

"I'm not doing this alone. Never alone."

Gabriel's eyes burned with emotion.

"You're not. And you never will."

Nathan nodded once.

Then he lifted the sword.

As he did—

The angels behind him lifted theirs.

In perfect unity.

As he did—

The angels behind him lifted theirs.

In perfect unity.

In perfect purpose.

In perfect silence.

And Michael's voice shook the foundations of the earth:

"ADVANCE."

The army of Heaven surged forward —and the Bridge, ancient and powerful and built to master worlds, realized with terrifying clarity:

It was about to face a force it had never accounted for— a force not of flesh, not of anomaly, not of the earth, but of God.

---

(29) THE END OF A THOUSAND SHADOWS

The earth groaned like something ancient and wounded.

Deep beneath the estate, in the lowest hollow where no human architect had ever walked, the Bridge fully revealed itself.

It was not a simple structure.

It was a *wound* in reality.

A sphere of stone and crystal sank into the foundations of the world, wrapped in bands of dull, pulsating light—like rings formed from trapped lightning and sorrow. Its surface moved as if it were muscle and stone at once, flexing, tightening, exhaling waves of invisible pressure. Dark veins of twisted energy, like black lightning, ran from it into the surrounding rock, forming a network that spidered toward distant places—toward cities, toward nations, toward unseen strongholds.

This was not just an object. It was a throne. A hub for principalities, a gathering place of powers and dominions whose hands had been in human suffering for centuries.

It pulsed again, sickly and insistent.

Hungry. Entitled. Certain.

Until the light arrived.

Nathan stepped into the cavern, and Heaven walked with him.

Behind him, the hosts of God poured through the opened veil like a river of fire and wings. Angels in ranks beyond counting, each armored in living light, swords drawn, faces set like flint.

Their presence filled the chamber with a holy pressure that made the air thrum, every breath feel heavy with glory.

Michael moved at Nathan's right again, sword unsheathed. Archangel Gabriel stood to his left, wings trailing light that shimmered across the cavern ceiling. The other archangels hovered nearby, forming a semi-circle around the human pair.

Human Gabriel.

Human Nathan.

Between them, the merged amulet glowed with a softer, gentler radiance.

A reminder: this was not just a war.

This was *love* coming to judge evil.

The Bridge reacted.

Dark energy surged up its veins, flaring in defiance. The bands around it constricted, glowing a toxic red. The air went colder, thick with the stench of spiritual rot—oppression, cruelty, fear. The accumulated residue of a thousand whispered lies across the ages.

It tried to loom. To impress. To intimidate.

Nathan did not move.

His armor shone with a clarity that no shadow could dim. The Sword of the Spirit burned in his hand, not with wild chaos, but with a steady, righteous flame.

The Bridge spoke, pressing its will into the cavern.

"You dare bring Heaven here?" it thundered, voice echoing in the walls and in the mind. "This is my domain. My crossing. My right."

Pain flickered in Nathan's chest at the pressure of it—but under that pain came something stronger.

A remembered truth.

For the weapons of our warfare are not of the flesh, but mighty through God to pull down strongholds…

Nathan lifted his head.

"No," he said, voice clear and resolute. "This was your cage. And your playground. But it was never your *right*."

The entity hissed, the bands contracting like the coils of a colossal serpent.

Gabriel stepped closer, the glow from Nathan's armor reflecting in his eyes.

"Nathan," he said softly, "you don't have to do this alone."

"I'm not alone," Nathan replied.

He tightened his grip on the sword.

"He's with me."

Nathan took a step forward.

The stone didn't just echo his footfall—it *responded*, lines of light rippling outward with each stride.

He squared his shoulders, eyes locked on the twisted, throbbing core of the Bridge.

"I will say this plainly," he declared, voice rising. "I am not God. I am not the Savior. I am not the Judge of all. But I belong to the One who *is*."

His voice rang through the cavern, amplified by something far greater than his own lungs.

"Every good thing," Nathan shouted, "comes from God—every perfect gift descends from Him! You have no claim on what belongs to Him!"

The Bridge shuddered.

The dark veins writhed, recoiling from the words as if they were acid.

He pressed on.

"I come against this power," Nathan declared, his words becoming like hammer blows, "this principality, this dominion. I come in the *Name above every name*."

The air quaked.

Michael raised his sword, angels following suit.

"In the mighty Name of Jesus Christ," Nathan roared, "I bring your works into the light, and I break them. I slice your authority. I cut your throne. I tear down the stones that are not laid by the hand of God Almighty!"

Light flared from his armor, stripping the cavern of shadows. Every dark corner lit. Every hidden crevice exposed.

The entity screamed. Not in sound alone, but in raw intention— in a thousand collapsed schemes, in a thousand interrupted plans.

"For millennia, I have ruled from beneath, my voice shrieked in the spiritual plane. *I have fed on fear, struck from darkness, twisted hearts, choked destinies—this is my power, this is my du—"*

"NO WEAPON," Nathan shouted, cutting through its rant, "formed against me shall prosper! Every tongue that has accused in judgment I bring to condemnation!"

The words crackled like a lightning strike.

The glow from his sword surged, its edges suddenly too bright to look at.

"No weapon," Nathan said again, lower now but somehow heavier, "formed against my family shall stand. Every tongue that has accused in judgment I bring to condemnation! No curse spoken against us shall hold. No plan of hell will outlive His decree."

He pointed the blade directly at the Bridge.

"You have tormented this world," he said, voice rough with fury and grief, "but your terror ends here. Not because of *me*—but because of the One whose word I carry."

He drew in a breath that tasted like iron and light.

Then he shouted, with every fiber of his being:

"In the Name of Jesus Christ, I strike you down to the pit of hell!"

He lunged.

The Sword of the Spirit came down and met the Bridge's outer band.

There was no clang.

No clash of metal.

The moment the sword touched it, the corrupted structure reacted like ice meeting boiling water.

It *screamed.*

The band shattered in a ring of collapsing light, chunks of stone and energy flying outward—but instead of falling, they dissolved into dust midair, consumed by the holiness pouring from the blade.

The entity convulsed.

"No—no—this crossing is MINE—"

Nathan advanced, the army of Heaven moving with him.

Angels surged forward, wings flaring, filling the cavern in a whirlwind of righteous fury. Some launched lances of pure light at the dark veins, severing them, closing pathways as they went. Others shielded Nathan and Gabriel from violent ripples of backlash—a storm of spiritual debris that would have obliterated mortal nerves if left unchecked.

The anomalies themselves stirred.

Fragments in their glass tubes cracked and burst free, not in rebellion, but in something like awe. Their luminous forms—their true selves long bound in scientific containers and spiritual agreements—rose like shimmering, translucent beings. Their essence vibrated in reverence at the Name Nathan had invoked.

Where once they had only guarded, watched, and bargained—

Now they *joined.*

They flung themselves at the remaining veins, funneling their energy into the weak points Nathan's sword had exposed, amplifying the damage.

The Bridge's consciousness writhed in disbelief.

"You betray your design!" it shouted at the anomalies. "You were built to preserve me!"

But their response, if it could be called that, was a single unified pulse directed toward Nathan:

"We stand with the Light. We are the rocks that cry out and proclaim praises to our Lord."

The entity shifted tactics.

The cavern flickered, overwhelmed by illusions—the ceiling turning to storms, the walls weeping faces, the floor splitting into chasms filled with every fear Nathan had ever carried.

Loss. Abandonment. Failure. Shame.

You are nothing. You are small. Who are you to speak for God?

Nathan staggered for half a heartbeat.

The Bridge pressed in—

—but another voice rose in him, deeper than his fear, older than his wounds:

"God has not given me a spirit of fear," Nathan said, his words steady as steel, "but of power, and love, and a sound mind. The Lord is my Shepherd. I know His voice. And you—" he lifted his head, eyes blazingly continued, "Have no authority here. Jesus Christ speaks in authority for me."

The words exploded from within him, not shouted this time, but *declared*.

The illusions shattered.

Storms vanished. Chasms sealed. Voices silenced.

What remained was simple and unmovable:

Stone. Light. The wounded world. And a human in radiant armor, standing between them and everything that wished them harm.

Nathan's eyes burned with a righteous and unextinguishable flame.

"I am *not* afraid of you," he said, voice steady. "Because the One in me is greater than anything in you."

He raised the sword again, flames of holy authority coiling along its length.

"You are not a god," The Bridge said. "You are not sovereign. You are not Lord."

He drew in one final breath.

"And every knee shall bow," he thundered, "and every tongue confess that *Jesus is Lord*—over earth, over heaven, and over *you*."

At that Name— truly, fully, unflinchingly spoken—

the Bridge broke.

Not just its shell. Not just its bands.

It's *right* to exist as a seat of oppression shattered.

Nathan lifted his voice again— not in fear, not in rage, but in the same covenant authority that once called fire down on Carmel and proved the Lord alone is God.

"God of Heaven," he declared, power rolling through every syllable, "Send Your holy fire— the fire that fell upon Elijah's sacrifice, the fire that consumes Your enemies yet shields Your beloved. The fire that walked with the three Hebrew boys.

Let that fire fall now. Let it strike this abomination— this living Bridge, this entity clothed in stone and shadow. Consume it. Destroy it. Vanquish it from the earth."

He didn't shout the last word. He released it, as though heaven breathed through him.

The ground answered.

A deep, resonant crack tore through the cavern, splitting stone from the heavens downward. Then another. And another— until the Bridge trembled like a living altar confronted by the true God.

The structure convulsed.

Brilliant white fissures raced through its form like living lightning. Dark veins—its channels of consciousness—lit up, burned, reversed, as if the very memory of its existence was being ripped from reality.

The Bridge screamed.

Not with the sound of collapsing stone, but with the raw, psychic agony of a creature being judged. Its voice was the shriek of every deception it had ever fed on. Every curse. Every hidden agreement. Every stronghold.

And they all shattered.

Nathan saw altars crumble. Contracts dissolve like ash. Chains splinter into dust. Every pathway this entity had ever opened— every tunnel of influence, manipulation, or oppression— collapsed in a single sweep of holy flame.

The wrath of God fell— not wild, not stray, but deliberate, precise, unstoppable.

The Bridge's last coherent thought was not defiance. It was a *shock*. "I never understood your love."

God's wrath tore through the Bridge-entity, leaving nothing standing that belonged to darkness. And when the last echo faded, the entire structure was gone— erased—as though it had never existed.

Silence thundered in the chamber.

Not the suffocating quiet of dread.

The deep, cleansing silence of something evil finally ended.

The broken core of the Bridge had not simply cracked; it had *ceased*. Where there had been a throbbing, malignant presence, there was now only stillness and stone—like a scar that had finally finished healing.

Nathan stood at the center of it all.

And he was… undeniably changed.

His armor, once blinding, settled into a soft, steady radiance—but his *body* had taken on the mark of where he'd just been. His hair, once its normal color, now flowed longer, touched by shimmering white, like he'd walked through a waterfall of light and it had decided to stay. Strands glowed faintly with a pearly luminescence, catching every glint of holiness still lingering in the air.

His face shone.

Not in a cartoonish way. In a way that made the lines of weariness smoother, the scars of old grief gentler, the gaze in his eyes clearer and brilliantly shining all the colors. It was the shine of someone who had stood in the presence of God and come back carrying a reflection of Him. Moses on the mountain—only now, wrapped in transparent armor and holding a sword of the living Word.

Gabriel stared.

"Nathan…" he whispered, voice shaking. "Your hair…"

Nathan reached up, touching it, fingers brushing the new length, the strange, silken texture.

He gave a breathless half-laugh.

"Well. That's… new."

"You're *glowing*," Gabriel said, unable to look away. "Your face… your hair… you look like—"

"A man who's been near the fire and didn't burn," Nathan finished softly. "I want to sometime tell you about those stories from a long time ago."

The angels hovered in formation, swords still drawn, scanning for any lingering residue. Finding none, they began to sing—not words, not in any human tongue, but pure sound, vibrating through stone and heart alike, washing the place clean.

Gabriel stared at Nathan with something approaching holy fear and tender love combined.

"I saw it," he whispered. "I saw… Him. Moving through you."

Nathan's eyes filled.

"It wasn't me," he said, voice unsteady. "I stood there. I swung. I spoke. But… it was never really me alone. It's *Him*. It's always Him."

Gabriel stepped forward and pulled him into his arms, armor and all.

"And I will testify," Gabriel said, voice broken with awed conviction, "for as long as I live, that I saw the power of God wielded through you to tear down an ancient terror. I will tell our son. I will tell our people. I will say: *I saw the Almighty move, and nothing stood in His way.*"

Nathan sheathed the sword. Even in its resting state, it hummed with restrained power.

Michael lowered his blade.

"The war under this place is finished," the archangel said. **"The mark of His glory remains upon you. It will never fade away."**

"The throne of oppression that once lay under this place is shattered. No tie remains. No chain will be reforged."

The host slowly began to withdraw, returning to the realms from which they had come—though several lingered around the couple, as if reluctant to leave them unguarded.

Michael turned his gaze on Gabriel.

"You, bloodline bearer," he said. **"You are charged: gather the scattered. Seek the remnant of your ancestors, the lost branches. Your son will lead them in days of peace yet to come."**

Gabriel's heart clenched.

"Tyler… will lead them?"

"He will grow into a man who knows peace because he saw war ended by love."

Michael's eyes softened. **"And he will shepherd a tribe reborn from fragments. This is decreed."**

He looked almost reverent as he said it.

Nathan's hair shifted as he turned—white, luminous, regal—and Gabriel realized with a strange, aching rush: His husband looked like a prince of another kingdom entirely.

"Those we find will see and know that what we tell them is the truth because the glory of God will be revealed and they will know of peace." Nathan said softly.

(30) MESSAGE OF PEACEMAKER

Night had fallen over their home.

Tyler sat on his bed with his duffel bag still half-zipped beside him, Claire on one side, Hailey pretending to be relaxed at the foot of the bed. The world outside his window looked normal. Ordinary.

His heart knew better.

The letter about Goldberg. The earlier message from Dad. The pressure in his chest that felt like something huge had just… broken.

Then, once again, the room filled with light.

This time it wasn't soft sunrise-gold. It was white. Pure. Layered with prismatic edges, like a diamond was breathing in the center of his room.

Claire grabbed the headboard.

Hailey whispered, "Okay, that's new—"

The light gathered, folding in on itself, shaping into a person.

Tyler's breath caught.

"Papa?"

The figure was changed.

It was Nathan. But not like Tyler had last seen him.

His hair was longer now, falling in soft, luminous waves just past his shoulders, washed through with radiant white as if every strand had been dipped in liquid moonlight. His face shone—not blinding, but undeniably bright, lines softened, eyes clear and deep, carrying something ageless behind the warmth.

A faint halo-like glow crowned his head and traced the edges of his armor, even though he was only half-there, spirit and body overlapping.

"Hey, little prince," Nathan said, smiling.

Tyler's jaw dropped.

"Papa Nathan… is that *you*?" he blurted. "You're glowing *white,* and your hair has changed, too! You look… You look *epic* and cooler!"

Nathan laughed, warm and genuinely delighted.

"I promise it's still me," he said. "Just… upgraded by the presence of God."

Hailey's eyes were huge and wet.

"Upgraded," she echoed faintly. "I'll say."

Claire wiped at her cheeks, torn between awe and tears.

"Nathan… what happened to you down there?" she whispered.

He looked at her gently.

"I stood in front of something old and cruel," he said, "and God stood in front of *me*. The rest is just… side effects."

He glanced back to Tyler, expression softening to that singular, father-heart focus that always made the boy feel like the only person in the world.

"The glow," Nathan said, tapping his own chest, "is just proof He's real, Ty. The power, the hair, the shine—it all comes from Him, not me."

Tyler grinned through his tears.

"You look like a warrior angel," he said.

Nathan's luminous eyes softened.

"I look like your Papa who just watched God end something ugly," he replied. "And I wanted *you* to see what His glory can do to a human heart that says 'yes.' I don't have long like this," Nathan said, "so I need you to listen with your heart."

Tyler nodded, body trembling.

Claire and Hailey listened too, hearts pounding.

"Tyler," Nathan said, and his voice changed—taking on a resonance that wasn't just his own anymore. "You are more than a child in this family story. You are more than the son of two men who love you. Heaven sees you. Heaven has plans for you."

Tyler's breath came fast and shallow.

"When you become a man," Nathan continued, "and when the time is right, you will find the woman meant to walk beside you. Together, you will not only build a family—you will *lead* one."

Images flickered in Tyler's mind as Nathan spoke:

A future version of himself, older, steady, standing among people whose faces bore similar eyes, similar bone structures, similar scars. A community restored. A tribe reborn.

"By God's hand," Nathan said, "your dad and I will track down the lost branches of his lineage. We will piece together the scattered tribe. We will bring them into one another's sight again."

The glow brightened.

"And *you*," Nathan said, voice thick with love, "will be their head. Not in pride. Not in cruelty. In peace."

Tears spilled down Tyler's cheeks.

"You will lead them in a time when the world is quieting from its storms," Nathan said. "You will be a man of peace after an age of war. God Himself will teach you what that means. You won't be perfect. But you will be *chosen* to guide. This isn't a chain," he added gently. "It's not a weight to crush you. It's a promise—that your life has purpose beyond fear. Beyond survival. You were born for more than just getting by. You were born for a time of rebuilding."

Claire and Hailey sat in stunned silence, tears streaking down their faces, not from fear—but from **hope**.

The glow around Nathan pulsed gently.

"I love you," he told them. "All of you. Remember—this light?" He gestured to himself, to his hair, his face. "It doesn't belong to me. It belongs to Him. And He's not done with any of us yet."

Tyler hiccupped, voice shaking.

"Papa… what if I mess it up?"

Nathan's glow warmed even more.

"Then grace will catch you," he said. "Just like it's catching me. Just like it's always caught us."

He lifted his gaze, encompassing Claire and Hailey.

"To you who stand with him," he said, "you are witnesses. Let these words root deep. Speak life over him when he doubts. Remind him of this night. Of this promise."

Claire nodded through tears.

"I will," she whispered. "I swear it."

Hailey's voice trembled. "Me too. I'm not going anywhere."

Nathan looked back at Tyler one last time.

"You are loved," he said. "You are covered. And you are not alone. In Christ, you are more than a conqueror. Don't forget that, okay?"

Tyler nodded so hard his hair flopped.

"I love you," Tyler choked out. "Please come home."

Nathan's smile wobbled.

"I will," he whispered. "Soon. And by the way, I love you the mostest."

Then the vision softened, the whiteness slowly dimming.

"Papa, don't go yet," Tyler whispered.

Nathan's smile was tender and unshaken.

"I'll see you soon, little prince," he said. "Walk in His peace. You're part of this light whether you glow or not."

And then he was gone.

But the memory of how he looked—regal, radiant, transformed—stayed burned into Tyler's mind, and the words saturated his heart because they were forged there in love.

None of this was meant as something terrifying. It was a picture of what it looks like when a human walks into the heart of darkness…with faith in God, and as a result comes back brighter.

In the forest outside Korinthos, Goldberg stood in a ring of broken branches and battered enemy gear, fists still clenched, chest heaving.

Across from him, a squad of elite operatives—emblem of the Obsidian Order stitched into their armor—regrouped under the trees.

"You're not getting past me," Goldberg growled, rolling his shoulders. "You want them, you go through *me*."

They began to advance—

—and vanished.

Just like that.

No flash. No noise. No theatrics.

One moment, they were coming. The next—gone.

Goldberg blinked.

He looked left. Right. Up to the sky.

"…Okay," he muttered. "Kinda rude."

He walked forward, prodding the air.

Nothing.

He huffed, half annoyed, half relieved.

"Spend all this time psyching myself up, and you don't even stick around to lose," he grumbled. Then softer, under his breath: "Guess somebody else finished the fight."

His shoulders slumped a little as the adrenaline faded, aches making themselves heard.

"I'm getting too old for this," he muttered. "I need a beach. And a drink. And about twelve naps."

Still, as he turned away from the empty battlefield, a small smile tugged at his lips.

"They're safe," he said. "That's what matters."

Back under the estate, the light began to calm.

The army of God slowly withdrew, leaving behind a cavern emptied of malice. No dark veins. No throbbing core. No hidden tunnels of oppression.

Just stone.

And the lingering echo of a Presence far greater than anything that had ever claimed this place before.

Nathan's armor dimmed to a steady radiance, not blinding—just quietly confident.

Gabriel took his hand.

"What now?" he whispered.

Nathan looked around the cavern that had once housed horror.

"Now," he said softly, "we live. We love. We build. We find your people. We raise our son. We walk in the peace He bought for us."

Michael watched them a moment longer, then inclined his head.

"The war under this place is finished," he said. "But the story above is just beginning."

Then he and the host were gone, leaving only a faint sweetness in the air and a warmth in the stone that would never quite fade.

Nathan and Gabriel stood alone, hand in hand, under an estate that no longer hid a monster.

Above them, the sky stretched clear.

Below them, no darkness lingered.

Between them, love held.

And somewhere far ahead, in a future only God could fully see, a grown Tyler would stand before his gathered people in a time of peace, leading them into a new era, carrying the legacy of two men who fought—and won—not by their strength alone, but by the power of the One who made them.

For now, though, there was this moment:

Quiet. Holy. Done.

Nathan exhaled.

"It's really over," he whispered.

Gabriel leaned his forehead against his.

"In Jesus' Name," he said softly, "it is."

And for the first time in a thousand years, The land beneath Korinthos rested.

(31) FOUNDATIONS FOR A FUTURE TRIBE

The estate felt *different* when they came back up.

The air in the old stone corridors no longer pressed in on them. The walls no longer hummed with the stale echo of something watching. Instead, there was a quiet warmth running under everything, like the afterglow of candles burned for the right reasons.

Gabriel walked slowly through the main hall, fingers trailing along the stones his ancestors had once feared. Nathan walked beside him, hair still washed in radiant white, armor now replaced with simple clothes—though nothing could hide the light that clung softly to his skin.

"Feels bigger," Nathan murmured.

"It's the same size," Gabriel said. "Just… not haunted anymore."

"Same thing," Nathan replied.

A team from a specialized historical restoration firm arrived within days—architects, engineers, preservationists, all of them briefed only on the *surface* details of the work. Gabriel walked them through each wing of the estate, explaining what should stay untouched, what should be fortified, and what needed to be reclaimed.

"The ancestral wing," he told them, standing in the long portrait corridor, "must remain structurally sound but unmodernized. We're not turning it into a hotel. This will be a place of memory. A place for my people to see where we came from."

The lead architect nodded, scribbling notes on a tablet.

"The lower levels?" she asked.

Gabriel and Nathan exchanged a glance.

"The cavern stays sealed to the public," Gabriel said firmly. "But not forgotten. We'll reinforce the access tunnel, create a guided route—one day. Not now. Eventually, it will be a place where we tell the story of what *used* to be down there… and what ended it."

Nathan added quietly, "And we're going to turn part of the underground space into storage, maybe living facilities, print shops, community centers, but…mostly storage."

"Storage?" the architect echoed.

"Storehouse," Nathan corrected gently. "A place for food. Supplies. Water purification systems. Emergency goods. If the world ever goes sideways again…" He glanced at Gabriel. "This estate will not be a monument to fear. It will be a refuge."

Gabriel nodded, something loosening in his chest.

Not a throne for terror. A base for blessing.

The architect scribbled faster.

"As for the other wings," Gabriel continued, "restore them completely. Guest suites. Community halls. Meeting rooms. Library spaces. We'll need a place big enough to hold a… very large family reunion."

Nathan bumped his shoulder lightly.

"Very," he said. "And some of them are probably loud."

Gabriel huffed a small laugh.

"I hope so."

They found the maps on their last night at the estate.

Not down in the cavern, not behind some secret panel, but in Gabriel's great-grandfather's study, tucked inside a flat, leather-bound case that had blended in with the other portfolios.

Nathan flipped it open and exhaled softly.

The inside was a layered atlas of a broken tribe.

There were world maps marked with tiny, precise ink lines. Some ran across continents, others through oceans, all ending in small red symbols Gabriel recognized from childhood stories—marks that meant *exile, dispersal, refuge.*

Each symbol had a note in the margin: a surname, a year, a phrase like "taken to commerce in the west" or "line absorbed into northern families" or simply "lost."

And then there were family trees.

Lines branched out from the Korinthos heartline—names, names, names, some circled, some crossed out, some marked with question marks where contact had been cut and never restored.

Gabriel's throat tightened.

"They tried," he whispered. "They tried to keep track of everyone. Even after… whatever horrors they were complicit in, they still—"

Nathan's fingers traced one of the missing branches.

"Then we finish what they couldn't," he said softly. "Not because of their guilt. Because of God's mercy."

On the final page, almost as an afterthought, was a note scrawled in their great-grandfather's uneven script:

If the Bridge ever falls, gather the scattered. If the flame ever rises, follow it to your people.

Gabriel touched the line with a reverent hand.

"The flame," he murmured.

Nathan's white hair caught the lamplight, glowing faintly.

"Make no mistake," Gabriel said, looking at him. "That's you."

Nathan bit back a smile. "Maybe you can affectionally call me the 'Torch' or 'Flickering Flame'? Still sounds a bit weird, like a dirty dancing dame. I got it, how about 'Nightlight'?"

"Ok, you can figure it out as we go. Let's burn through some distance," Gabriel chuckled at Nathan's clown-like faces…"We do this together, carefully, Bozo."

On their last walk through the estate before leaving, they tested what had changed.

Nathan stood on the balcony overlooking the valley, eyes closed. He whispered a simple request under his breath—for the wind to shift, for a storm cloud gathering on the horizon to reroute away from a nearby village.

When he opened his eyes, the cloud turned as if obeying a quiet command. Not violently, not unnaturally. Just… gently re-guided.

Gabriel watched, arms folded.

"Show-off," he said softly.

"You're one to talk," Nathan replied.

Gabriel focused on a boulder at the far edge of the grounds—one that would have taken heavy machinery to move. With a thought, he lifted it, not straining, not sweating. It simply rose, hung in the air, then drifted silently to a different spot. He set it down as softly as if it were a teacup.

When he turned back, Nathan was staring—not in fear, but in open, delighted wonder.

"We were strong before," Nathan said. "This is… more."

Gabriel sobered.

"It's not for showing off," he said. "You know that."

"I know." Nathan nodded, expression earnest. "It's for finding people. For protecting them. For feeding them. For rebuilding. This isn't about being superhuman. It's about being *responsible*."

Gabriel stepped closer, cupping the side of his face.

"'To whom much is given…'"

"…much is required," Nathan finished the Spiderman quote quietly. "I remember."

The amulet pulsed between them—stronger than ever, but peaceful now.

The private jet cut through the clouds on the way back, sun painting the wings in gold.

Nathan sat by the window, white hair almost merging with the brightness. Gabriel sat beside him, hand linked with his, thumb tracing calming circles over his skin.

"Are you ready?" Nathan asked.

"For what?"

"For Tyler, seeing you after all this."

Gabriel smiled softly.

"I'm more worried about him seeing *you*," he said. "You look like you just finished a yearlong worship session in the throne room."

"You say that like it's a bad thing."

"It's not." Gabriel's eyes warmed. "It's beautiful. It's just… a lot to take in that with the new powers and the present reminder of what happened."

Nathan looked down at their joined hands.

"It *is* a lot," he admitted. "But God didn't do this to make me untouchable. He did it so I could touch more—reach farther, lift heavier, love stronger. I'm still me."

Gabriel squeezed.

"Good," he murmured. "Because I fell in love with *you*, not a glowstick."

Nathan snorted and lightly smacked the shoulder of Gabriel. Gabriel mused and gently rubbed his shoulder as if in hiding pain.

By the time the jet landed, a crowd had gathered on the private tarmac—Henrik, Hailey, Claire, and Tyler in front, Goldberg slightly back with his arms crossed, pretending he wasn't as emotional as the rest.

The door opened.

Nathan stepped out first, more like FLASH, and then floated out first.

Tyler's eyes went *wide*.

"PAPA NATHAN!" he shouted. "You're still glowing! And your hair is even cooler in sunlight!"

Nathan barely landed at the end of the steps before Tyler launched himself at him. Nathan caught him easily, spinning once, the boy's laughter bubbling over.

"I missed you," Tyler said into his shoulder.

"I missed you, too," Nathan whispered. "More than you know."

Gabriel descended after, and Claire reached for him, pulling him into a tight, somewhat teary hug.

"You brought him home," she whispered, looking at Nathan.

"We both came home," Gabriel answered, glancing at Nathan too, and relieved, "By grace."

Hailey punched Nathan lightly in the arm the second she got close enough.

"You look like you walked out of a Christian fantasy novel," she sniffed. "I approve."

Henrik adjusted his glasses, looking between Nathan's glowing countenance and Gabriel's calm, grounded presence.

"I knew leaving you two unsupervised would change the world," he muttered. "Didn't expect the *hair*, though."

Then Goldberg stepped forward.

He gave Nathan a long, appraising stare.

"You look weird, kid," he said.

Nathan grinned. "A good weird?"

Goldberg's mouth twitched.

"The kind of weird that makes demons rethink their life choices," he said. "I'll take it."

He pulled Nathan into a rough one-armed hug, then Gabriel into another, smacking his back just a little too hard.

"You did well," Goldberg murmured. "Proud of you both."

It was Henrik who screamed first.

Not in fear. In overwhelmed, spreadsheet-shattering joy.

They were barely back in their home office when he burst in, hair a mess, tablet in hand.

"Okay," he said, voice an octave too high, "so while you two were busy smiting cosmic evil and having supernatural hair makeovers, God appears to have hijacked the global economy on your behalf."

Nathan blinked.

"…come again?"

Henrik shoved the tablet between them.

"Every company Gabriel had even a *minor* stake in? Exploded. In a good way. Market surges that make no sense. Properties tied to your charitable shell entities? Tripled in value. Patents you filed for energy, water purification, sustainable tech? Approved and fast-tracked with endorsement. Anomalies cleaned up corrupted financial records, and everything honest you touched—just… boomed."

Gabriel frowned slightly.

"How much are we talking?"

Henrik's eye twitched.

"You're… um… past billionaire. Past multi-trillionaire." He swallowed. "You've crossed theoretical economic models. You're in quadrillion territory. Plural."

Silence.

Nathan stared.

Gabriel raised an eyebrow.

Goldberg from the doorway muttered, "Well, damn."

Hailey leaned in.

"So… we're tithing *big*, right?"

Nathan sat down slowly.

"This isn't for us," he said softly. "We can't even pretend. This is for *them*."

Gabriel nodded, mind already racing—not with luxuries, but with possibilities.

"Churches that need roofs," he murmured. "Food banks that need supply chains. Areas hit by storms that never recover. Orphanages. Schools. Micro-loans. Entire regions that could be lifted."

Henrik's eyes shimmered.

"We can build systems that live beyond us," he said. "Foundations that cannot be bought. Transparency, integrity, long-term sustainability. Money as a *tool* instead of a god."

Nathan smiled faintly.

"Exactly. The only God in this story isn't in the bank."

That night, Nathan sat with Gabriel on their balcony, city lights twinkling below.

"So," Gabriel said carefully, "what about Disney?"

Nathan exhaled, watching the stars.

"I still love it," he said. "I still want to finish what I started. The Enchantment Realm deserves to be completed. Kids deserve a place where they feel like magic and goodness are possible. But…"

"But?"

"It's not my *whole* calling anymore," Nathan admitted. "I've seen too much now. Felt too much. I can't pour all of myself into crowds and fireworks when there are people starving, families fractured, and your tribe waiting to be found."

Gabriel nodded slowly.

"What are you thinking?" he asked.

Nathan turned toward him.

"I'll finish the park," he said. "All of it. Every detail we dreamed of. I'll open it, celebrate it, and hand it off." He smiled, tired but content. "And then I step down. Let Henrik or someone we trust step into the role. I'll stay as a consultant if they want. But my full-time heart?" He tapped his chest. "It's supposed to be… out there now."

He gestured at the world beyond their balcony.

"Finding your people," Nathan continued. "Resourcing God's dreams for the poor and broken. Teaching others that family is something you *build* and protect, not just something you're born into."

Gabriel's eyes glistened.

"Are you sure?" he whispered. "Disney was your star when you were ten."

Nathan's white hair shimmered as he leaned forward, resting his forehead against Gabriel's.

"You were my star when I was grown," he answered. "And God lit something even bigger behind you. My dream changed. That's allowed."

Gabriel let out a soft, shaky laugh.

"Okay, Foreign Fire. Let's light the way."

In the days that followed:

- Lawyers were quietly instructed to divest certain assets and create sprawling, heavily-protected charitable trusts.
- Anonymous donations began reshaping cities, programs, and small communities with almost surgical precision.
- Plans for a reconstructed estate in Korinthos were drawn up, with entire wings designated for future family gatherings, counseling centers, and cultural archives.
- An entire department formed overnight, dedicated to tracking down Gabriel's scattered lineage using the maps and family trees they'd uncovered.

Goldberg settled into the role of "grumpy uncle who knows too much," alternating between training security teams and complaining about needing a beach vacation.

Hailey and Henrik found themselves co-managing half a dozen new initiatives—mock-bickering while secretly thriving on the sense of purpose.

Tyler started sleeping with one hand over his heart, where he imagined his own invisible armor would one day form.

Nathan and Gabriel prayed together more.

Not because they were afraid.

Because they knew what it meant now to carry this much power, this much favor, this much responsibility.

For the first time in a long time, the horizon ahead of them wasn't dark with looming dread.

It was wide. Bright. Open.

There were scars. There were ghosts in memory. There were missing people whose names they hadn't learned yet.

But now there was time. Resources. Calling.

And a God who had proven, unmistakably, that no principality, no dominion, no throne built in secret could stand when His people called on His Name and refused to bow.

Nathan glanced at Gabriel one quiet morning and said, almost to himself:

"The Bridge is gone. But our bridges are just starting."

Gabriel smiled.

"And this time," he replied, "they'll only ever carry love."